# TRACK DOWN THAILAND

*A Brad Jacobs Thriller*

## *Book 8*

**SCOTT CONRAD**

**PUBLISHED BY:**
Scott Conrad
Copyright © 2020
**All rights reserved.**

No part of this publication may be copied, reproduced in any format, by any means, electronic or otherwise, without prior consent from the copyright owner and publisher of this book.

This is a work of fiction. All characters, names, places and events are the product of the author's imagination or used fictitiously.

Scott Conrad's "A Brad Jacobs Thriller" Series takes retired Force Recon Marine Brad Jacobs and his fellow veterans on dangerous and thrilling international search, rescue and hostage retrieval expeditions. Their missions are to "Track Down" and retrieve innocent victims by facing off against fierce, powerful enemies and extremely challenging conditions.

Enjoy the non-stop action, adventure and mystery with the entire team as they always manage to keep their sense of humor even during the riskiest of operations. Each book is a complete story on its own.

*A Brad Jacobs Thriller Series by Scott Conrad:*

**TRACK DOWN AFRICA – BOOK 1**
**TRACK DOWN ALASKA – BOOK 2**
**TRACK DOWN AMAZON – BOOK 3**
**TRACK DOWN IRAQ – BOOK 4**
**TRACK DOWN BORNEO – BOOK 5**
**TRACK DOWN EL SALVADOR – BOOK 6**
**TRACK DOWN WYOMING – BOOK 7**
**TRACK DOWN THAILAND – BOOK 8**

Visit the author at: ScottConradBooks.com

*"Freedom is not free, but the U.S. Marine Corps will pay most of your share."*

**Captain J.E. "Ned" Dolan, USMC (Ret.) Platoon Leader E/27, Korean War.**

# Table of Contents

PROLOGUE ........................................................................ 1

Chapter One .................................................................... 7

Chapter Two ...................................................................19

Chapter Three ................................................................33

Chapter Four ..................................................................49

Chapter Five ...................................................................69

Chapter Six .....................................................................88

Chapter Seven.............................................................. 107

Chapter Eight ............................................................... 117

Chapter Nine................................................................ 147

Chapter Ten .................................................................. 164

Chapter Eleven ............................................................ 180

Chapter Twelve ............................................................ 190

Chapter Thirteen .........................................................213

Chapter Fourteen ........................................................228

Chapter Fifteen.............................................................255

Chapter Sixteen ...........................................................270

| | |
|---|---|
| Chapter Seventeen | 284 |
| Chapter Eighteen | 306 |
| Chapter Nineteen | 321 |
| Chapter Twenty | 339 |
| Chapter Twenty-one | 362 |
| Epilogue | 385 |

# PROLOGUE

## Mountains east of Tambon Ban Bueng, Ban Kha District, Ratchaburi, Thailand, four years ago.

Kirill Bykov, former Polkovnik in the Foreign Intelligence Service of the Russian Federation (SVR, Sluzhba vneshney razvedki Rossiyskoy Federatsii), was responsible for wet work (foreign assassinations), primarily along the Sino-Soviet border, which had been a constant but little known shooting war for more than fifty years. He had run afoul of his superiors and left the service of Mother Russia, gravitating first to the newborn Russian Mafia and then branching out on his own.

With a cadre of former Zhonghu Rénmín Jiěfàngjūn tèzhǒng bùduì (the special forces of the Chinese People's Liberation Army (PLA), which he laughingly referred to as his cultural aides) along with three trusted subordinates from the SVR, a captain (Kapitan Mikhail Orel) and two senior sergeants (Starshiy Serzhant Vassily Moroz and Demyan Chorney), he was preparing to overrun a monastery in the mountains forty miles outside Tambon Ban Bueng. The monastery was the home of a sect of renegade Buddhist monks that had been ostracized and shunned by the other orders.

The monastery itself was spacious, covering some sixty hectares, and had a large and relatively modern central complex that Bykov felt was ideal for his purposes. It was fairly close to Bangkok and Ko Phai Island, where he had purchased an exclusive high-end resort with funds he'd raised selling arms as a Russian Mafia don. The international arms market had become far too cutthroat and competitive, and Bykov was aging. He had formulated a plan for a lucrative and far less risky enterprise, the kidnapping of the wives and daughters of the ultra-rich. The potential profits were enormous, and he planned to be judicious in selecting his victims.

*Scott Conrad*

\* \* \*

Thirty former members of China's premier Special Forces unit, clad in night camouflage and heavily armed, lay in a three-hundred-sixty-degree circle at their ORP (objective rally point). Every third man carried a great coil of climbing rope with a folding grappling hook attached to one end. They were waiting for the recon team to return with final confirmation as to the disposition of the monks in the monastery.

The monks themselves were of a militant renegade sect that had taken the martial arts at the core of their religion to a level much higher than the rest of their order had and as a result had been first disciplined and then shunned by their peers. After losing their financial backing from the order, the renegades took things a bit further and began to hire themselves out to perform services they were uniquely capable of performing. It was a prime example of religion gone bad. Theft, kidnapping, even assassinations were performed quickly, quietly, and, most of all, inconspicuously. It was said that even the least skilled of the monks could make a true ninja look like a rank amateur ... and it was all done without the use of firearms. Firearms were proscribed by the sect, and that was a key element of Kirill Bykov's assault plan.

The recon team approached the ORP as noiselessly as a shadow, with the point man creeping to within five meters of the perimeter. A challenge was issued followed by the correct password and the recon team was permitted reentry. The recon team hastily confirmed the original intel and Bykov gave the go-ahead for the assault.

Their instructions were simple and concise. The assault team would separate into four elements with three ten-man teams scaling the craggy peak to the monastery and the fourth securing a perimeter at the base of the peak acting as a reserve. With a hand signal, Bykov initiated the assault ... that was the only way to describe it. The mission was to eliminate every living occupant inside the monastery. Bykov did not want anyone left to organize or even attempt to recapture the personal fortress he already envisioned the ancient monastery to be.

After the few monks serving as sentries were taken out by a handful of 'cultural aides' cross-trained by Ghurka troops on loan from Nepal, the rest of the monks were taken by surprise; the AK-74-armed intruders executed a bloodbath, following Bykov's instructions to the letter. When it was over, the only things alive inside the massive building were the intruders themselves. Among them was Bykov himself. Despite his age, he was incredibly fit, and he had scaled the ropes just as his men had done. Kirill Bykov led by example.

Bykov sent a delegation of his 'cultural aides' to China to bring back a crew of Chinese villagers to clean up the mess. The local villagers were terrified of the mad Russian, but they weren't so scared that they refused to do business with him or provide him the services he required. Bykov was meticulous in his dealings with the local populace, careful to pay well and on time for whatever he received … but he was not a man to tolerate being cheated. He tended to make an example of anyone who tried to cheat him.

Once the monastery had been cleared of any trace of its occupation by the monks, a construction crew was secretly brought in from Malaysia at enormous expense. The monastery was transformed, renovated and modernized by a construction contractor to some very exacting specifications, totally in secret. The project took three years and cost multiple millions of euros.

Outside, it appeared the same as it had for centuries. Inside, it was luxurious and ultramodern. Kirill Bykov was ready and open for business.

# Chapter One

**Ko Phai Island, Bay of Bangkok, one year ago.**

Emily Larroquette, the exotically beautiful young jet-set daughter of Clarence Larroquette, was spoiled rotten. Her father was an oil rich multi-billionaire whose fortune had been made brokering oil deals between Nigeria and India. From the day she was born she'd been indulged in every way by her father, who spared no expense when it came to pleasing his daughter. He could refuse her nothing.

Before she could even walk, he hired a team of bodyguards to protect her. As she grew older, Clarence was careful to select women who were classy enough to dance attendance on Emily in the poshest of social circles yet deadly enough to kill with their bare hands. Her current protectors were a pair of South African beauties who just incidentally happened to be world-class martial artists and former mercenaries.

After a wild two-week cruise in the Aegean Sea with her friends, Emily decided that she needed to spend a week or so at the ultra-exclusive Khwām Sukh (Pleasures) Spa, for women only, on the island of Ko Phai in the Bay of Bangkok, Gulf of Siam. While on the cruise, she'd overheard some positively lascivious gossip about the ultra-high-end resort that appealed to her ... prurient interests. As his daughter was never one to miss an opportunity to exercise those interests, Clarence Larroquette had spent a fortune keeping her name out of the news. Emily did take time to call Sarah, her daddy's secretary, so he would know where she was going to be before she made the reservations. She made the reservations for herself, her best friend and partner in crime Mimi Cardone, and her bodyguards at the resort. The bill, of course, was charged to Daddy's American Express Centurion card. She and Mimi planned to make extensive use of the spa facilities there, particularly the more exotic features.

\* \* \*

Within an hour of her arrival, Emily had managed to spend more than twenty-five thousand dollars of her daddy's money in the gift shop. First she had seen a microkini that she just had to have. Then she decided that Mimi should get one as well (but not as tiny as the one she had gotten, Emily did not like to share the spotlight). Of course, her bodyguards needed swimsuits as well, but she bought plain one-piece suits for them.

"I don't know about you, Mimi, but I'm headed for that gorgeous pool!" Emily had put on the tiny string bikini that revealed an incredible expanse of smooth, tanned, and pampered skin. Slipping on a white, monogrammed terry cloth robe provided by the resort for the convenience of their guests, she moved toward the door of her suite, her movements sinuous and feline.

Mimi followed her. She had read the brochures, and she knew that the waiters around the pool were all male—and from what she had seen, they were all absolutely gorgeous. The girls she and Emily had overheard on the cruise had tittered and giggled as they described the pool waiters and their (according to them) willingness to serve the guests in any way they could. She'd heard even more gossip about the masseurs, but she hadn't been sure that had been credible. One thing she knew for certain; Emily would do everything in her power to find out if the gossip was true or not. There was nothing shy or bashful about her friend.

"I think I'd like another of those fabulous rum drinks, Jason, you know; the ones with the little parasols in them." She batted her long eyelashes at the nearly naked bronzed Adonis holding a tray in his hand, a small white monogrammed towel across his arm. He smiled down at her, flashing smooth, even white teeth. Emily's glance dropped to his midsection, barely covered by a loincloth that left the tanned skin of his thighs and hips bare and lingered there for a long time before he turned and walked over to the bar to get her drink.

"Hey, he didn't even ask if I wanted anything!" Mimi said, pouting.

"You get your own waiter, Mimi, you know that," Emily said, sitting up in her chaise lounge and reaching up behind her back with both hands, an act only women seem to be able to perform, and untied the spaghetti strings that held her bikini top in place. The miniscule piece of fabric fluttered to her lap when she shrugged her shoulders, leaving her breasts completely bare. They had been informed in the lobby that waiters were assigned to each chair around the enormous eccentrically shaped pool. There were also more than a dozen private cabanas around the perimeter of that pool as well, and it was not uncommon to see a waiter escorting a guest into one of them, dropping the gauzy entrance curtains behind them.

Mimi wasn't scandalized by Emily's actions, she was used to them. During their Aegean cruise it had not been unusual to see Emily strip off all her clothes and dive overboard to frolic with the other passengers every time the large wooden sailing vessel dropped anchor.

Jason returned with Emily's drink, stopping in front of her and bowing down so that she wouldn't have to reach for it. If he noticed that she had removed her top, he gave no indication of it.

"Is there anything else I can do for you, ma'am?" He was very polite, even obsequious. Mimi was amused … Emily was not.

"Yes," she purred. "I'm getting a lot of sun. Would you please put some lotion on me?" With an enigmatic smile on her face, she leaned back in the chaise and spread her arms.

* * *

Bykov leaned back in the custom-built Eames chair and put his elegantly shod feet up on the surface of his highly polished, hand-built Brazilian rosewood desk. He was staring intently at a large computer monitor. The monitor displayed, on command, the video output of any of the security cameras in the monastery (which he had whimsically named Logovo, the Russian word for 'lair') or a dozen of them at once. Logovo was riddled with hundreds of concealed wireless Relohas HD 1080P Spy Cameras with live streaming, upgraded night vision, and motion activation capabilities. Chinese technicians had altered the devices so that they could be hardwired into the electrical system instead of requiring periodic battery changes.

The system worked so well that he made sure to have the same equipment installed in his Pleasures Spa on Ko Phai Island. He switched his monitor over to the live spa feed. The images currently being displayed were from the pool deck. He'd been flashing through the cameras when the sight of Emily Larroquette removing her microkini top caught his eye. He had quickly isolated and enlarged the display and leaned back to enjoy the sight. The woman was magnificent, and she was a coquette par excellence.

"There, Mikhail! Pull up the background file for that woman and send it to my screen. Instantly, a box opened, inset into the bottom of the camera display. Kapitan Mikhail Orel began to read the contents of the file, unnecessarily translating it from Russian into English.

"Emily Jane Larroquette, twenty-three. Only child of Clarence Harding Larroquette, multi-billionaire oil broker, specializes in negotiating bulk oil contracts between Nigeria and India. Spends most of the year traveling. No mother. The father dotes on the girl and spares no expense when covering her indiscretions. She's a prime candidate, fits the profile perfectly, from a financial standpoint anyway." Mikhail had gone to Northwestern

University in Chicago for his undergraduate degree, courtesy of the SVR. He spoke like the La Salle Street stockbroker he could have been. Bykov had long been accustomed to the Americanisms in Orel's English.

Bykov watched as Emily stretched lazily and ran her hand up Jason's bare thigh and under his loincloth before standing up and leading him to one of the cabanas. She was precisely the kind of woman he was looking for to start his new business enterprise with. She would also provide an interesting diversion for an evening ... her beauty alone justified that. She was not, however, to his tastes. He preferred a woman who was not quite so easily taken to bed. A man had to maintain his standards, after all.

"Observe this woman, Mikhail. She is exactly the type of woman we need to identify and then cultivate for our new venture." He crossed his hands behind his neck, leaned back in his plush, custom-built chair and sighed in satisfaction as Mikhail Orel accessed the security camera program and isolated the pool cam.

"She is a bit of a flirt, sir." Orel was master of the understatement.

"Very much so, I'm happy to say."

"Do you want me to lay on the chopper for tonight, sir?"

"No, Mikhail. We must bide our time with this first one, we have come too far and invested too much of my capital to risk making an error with the very first of our targets. I need to wine her and dine her a bit before I lure her out to Logovo, give her a false sense of security."

"Forgive me for pointing out the obvious, sir, but we also need to address the issue of the bodyguards and the friend. Once this one is missing those three will raise the alarm and notify the father ... and the authorities."

"I've already considered that. When the time comes, Miss Larroquette will think she is off on an adventure and will be delighted to give her caretakers and friend the slip. She will be a willing dupe, Mikhail." He thought for a moment. "I will decide how to handle the bodyguards before we make our move; just focus on ways to attract more like her to Pleasures."

It was Orel's turn to lean back in his chair and think. After several minutes he spoke again. "Will we be taking a small group this first time, sir?"

Bykov sighed. His number two was a brilliant logistician and assistant, but one of the qualities that made him such a jewel of an assistant was also his biggest flaw. He was too eager.

"Not now, Mikhail. She is only booked for a two-week stay, and we must take our time. We are not ready. I need time to work out all of the details. We will lure her back for a return visit when the time is right. Consider this to be what you would call a trial run ... and she will be the only one this time. I need you to hone your skills in identifying the likeliest of our guests for our venture."

Bykov turned back to his computer monitor and resumed spying upon his guests.

# Chapter Two

**Jacobs Ranchette, northwest of Dallas, Texas, present day.**

Vicky Chance, a very tall and deceptively slender woman with long red hair, green eyes, and legs that seemed to go on forever, did not want to admit that she was exhausted after Team Dallas' mission to Wyoming's Wind River Range. The truth was that there had been precious little time between missions since she had joined the team in Mexico, and the exhaustion was a cumulative product of the missions.

When she first met Brad Jacobs and the rest of Team Dallas, she had been an I.C.E. agent for the Department of Homeland Security investigating child exploitation and trafficking in the Southern Cone. Before that she had been a United States Marine Corps Criminal Investigation Division (USMC C.I.D.) warrant officer CW03. Jacobs, taken by her looks at first, was even more taken with her skills after their joint mission to the Amazon and had offered her a spot on Team Dallas.

Now she lived with Jacobs on a sprawling ranchette northwest of Dallas, Texas. She had come to care for him deeply, but she was very cautious about tossing the "L" word around too casually. The plain truth was that even in the Army there had been stand downs and annual leave. She needed a break, somewhere she could relax and be pampered. Even between missions, there was an enormous amount of work that had to be performed so that Team Dallas could function at maximum efficiency.

Sighing, she glanced over at Brad's cousin Jessica Paul, who was still limping slightly from an ankle injury—it had been a sprain instead of a fracture—that she'd picked up when they had haloed into Wind River Range to bring ordnance and communications gear to Brad and two other members of Team Dallas, Mason Ving and Jared Smoot. The three men had actually been on a vacation of sorts, roughing it, fishing and hunting, when they had spotted a celebrity multibillionaire being chased down and kidnapped.

The two women were sitting in lawn chairs on the back patio of the ranch house, catching a few rays of the hot Texas sun and sipping iced tea from tall, frosty glasses along with most of the other members of Team Dallas. Jessica, a long, cool blonde with an athletic body, was rubbing suntan lotion on her long, shapely legs. Before she had bullied her way onto Team Dallas, forcing her cousin Brad to recognize her innate capabilities and her reliability in combat, she had been an adventuress and treasure hunter; her facility for languages and her cool-headedness under fire had proven an invaluable asset to the team.

"This is nice, but I think I need a vacation, Jess…"

"Yeah," Jessica replied. "Me too. Someplace swanky where I could be pampered and spoiled, my every whim catered to." She said it in such a sardonic tone that everyone present sailed off into gales of laughter. An outsider observing the little vignette would never have guessed that both these beautiful women were battle-hardened veterans of the kind of real-life combat usually depicted in action/adventure movies.

Brad, whose large hand encompassed a Lone Star beer instead of an iced tea glass, smiled over at Vicky with genuine affection.

"What? You two act like we didn't come back from a sweet vacation in Wyoming's magnificent Wind River Range!"

"Sweet vacation my butt!" Vicky retorted. "A night halo jump followed by stumbling up a rocky mountainside and re-enacting Custer's Last Stand is not my idea of a 'sweet' vacation."

Jessica didn't find Brad's comment as amusing as Vicky had.

"Doing all that with an ankle swollen to the size of a basketball was just loads of fun. Gee Brad, can we do it again?" Her voice was dripping with good-natured sarcasm.

"Awww, ladies, ladies! Don't let a coupla little hitches like that spoil the memory of them gorgeous mountains an' them beautiful blue lakes ... an' them fishes!" Mason Ving, an enormous jet black man with bulging muscles and a shiny bald pate, had served with Brad in Iraq and Afghanistan in Force Recon, the elite force of the United States Marines.

"Golden trout," Brad proffered, raising his Lone Star into the air in a mock toast.

"Don't tease them, Ving." Willona Ving spoke over the rim of her tea glass. "There are grown men out there that can't do whatever it is you boys do, and you know it. You ought to be ashamed of yourselves." She glared first at her husband then at Brad.

"Not that I don't adore every one of you, but it does get a little old just hanging around you guys twenty-four seven, you know," Vicky said, her sultry eyes locked on Brad. "Not to mention the fact that every time we go on a mission it seems that most of us come back hurt in one way or another. I'm not complaining, but sometimes I just want to do things and have conversations that make me feel ... I don't know ... girly. You guys went off to Wyoming for some 'guy' time. I think Jess and I should take a little vacation time too."

Brad set his Lone Star down beside his lawn chair.

"So why don't you? Go find yourself some place that caters to women only and have yourself a ball. Hell, you've more than earned it." He swiveled his head until he was facing Willona, recently appointed treasurer for Team Dallas. "You too,

Willona. Our coffers are full right now. They can stand footing the bill for a resort or a spa, can't they?"

"We sure can, Brad Jacobs, but I'm not going to go away and leave my two boys under the not-so-watchful eyes of you outlaws!" She was smiling, and that took the sting out of her words. "I would stay right here and make sure they didn't pick up any bad habits." Willona was determined that Jordan and Nathaniel would not follow in their father's footsteps. She loved Ving with all her heart, but she did not love his profession.

Brad turned back to Vicky and Jessica.

"Where would you like to go? Hawaii? Fiji? The Seychelles?"

Willona interrupted.

"Just this week I was reading about a very exclusive resort, just for women. The place is unbelievable! From everything I read, you get the royal treatment from the moment you set foot on the property. Everything is covered except the gift shop, all included in a package. The employees are not even permitted to take gratuities! It's on an island in the Gulf of Siam, part of Thailand if I remember correctly."

"That's ridiculous!" Vicky was chuckling. "It probably costs a small fortune to stay there, and that's not even counting the cost of flying halfway around the world to get there. Just let me think on it a little while. I'm sure there's someplace a hell of a lot closer and less expensive to go to."

"Compared to what these men had to pay for all the hunting and fishing licenses, fees—and that mission you all managed to 'stumble' into, it wouldn't be as bad as you'd think," Willona retorted. She neglected to mention the very substantial reward Nicholas Ainsley had paid, unasked, to Team Dallas once he'd been rescued;

that had been far more than enough to cover the expenses Team Dallas had incurred. Grateful billionaires were turning out to be surprisingly generous.

"I don't think it's such a ridiculous idea," Jessica said. "Willona, what's the name of that place?"

"It's called Khwām Sukh, that's 'Pleasures' in Thai."

"And where did you say it was?"

"It's on the island of Ko Phai in the Bay of Bangkok."

Jessica made a mental note to check out the particulars of the resort. Thailand was a country she'd never been to before, and the adventuress in her adored—no, craved—new sights and exploring new cultures. A visit to Pleasures might be just what the doctor ordered. It would be nice, for a change, to go somewhere there was no one trying to kill her.

*Track Down Thailand*

\* \* \*

Jessica sat curled up with her laptop on the living room sofa in the Dallas apartment she shared with her boyfriend and fellow Team Dallas member Charlie Dawkins. Charlie, a six-foot rawboned Texan with coal-black hair, blue eyes, and big hands, had been recruited to Team Dallas after the successful mission to Alaska. He'd been on an assignment for the Department of State's enforcement arm when he'd been flying to Stephan Lake Lodge in Talkeetna, Alaska with Pete Sabrowski, a longtime friend and, incidentally, a Team Dallas member. The bush plane they had chartered for the trip to the lodge had gone down, and Charlie had ended up working with Team Dallas on a joint operation. Jessica had taken to him right away, and he had earned the respect of the team when the chips were down.

"What are you doing, baby?"

Jessica looked up from her laptop, gazing fondly and a little lasciviously at her live-in boyfriend. He was fresh from the shower and only wore a damp towel low-slung around his hips.

"I'm looking up a resort Willona told us about this afternoon. You've got to look at this, this place is absolutely incredible!" She slid the laptop slightly to one side and patted the sofa cushion beside her. Freshly washed man was a scent Jessica loved, especially when that man was Charlie.

He leaned against her and checked out the website displayed on the laptop screen and let out a low whistle.

"That's some place!" He leaned against the back of the sofa and Jess felt a small pang of loss as he did so. "So, when do we go?"

Jessica smiled at him.

"Read again, baby. No boys allowed."

"Ahhh, you're going to leave me…"

"Vicky wants a vacation, a break, and I do too. We haven't had any girl time in ages. We were talking about it up at Brad's house today and Willona suggested this place. I've got to say, she was right; it really looks awesome."

He smiled and slid his arm around her shoulder, pulling her close.

"And what am I supposed to do while you're off halfway across the world?" He kissed her forehead.

"You'd better rest up for when I get back," she quipped, a sly smile on her lips. "I need some girly time, but I have a feeling I'm going to be quite ready for some of the personal attention you're so good at…"

\* \* \*

"If they decide to go, Fly, would you like to go with them?" Fly was Felicity Highsmith, a retired technical wizard with deep ties to the U.S. intelligence community. Felicity Marie Highsmith had earned her first doctorate from MIT at the age of sixteen. A child prodigy, she had earned her second doctorate before she was eighteen. Highly recruited by the National Security Agency (NSA), she'd spent twenty-one years with that organization, the last eleven coordinating highly classified intelligence between all the different intelligence agencies and departments of the Federal government. At the age of thirty-nine, against the wishes and the extraordinary efforts of her superiors, Felicity retired, weary of the games and the bullshit of the D.C. bureaucracy.

She provided all the fascinating new high-tech gadgets that were proving so useful in completing their missions. She was the only member of Team Dallas who was a non-combatant. Deeply involved in their missions now, she maintained their communications links and the videos from her drones via satellite links, giving real-time intelligence that had saved their asses more than once in the brief time she had been a team member. In short, she had become essential.

"Oh hell no, Brad! I'm working on some new software that will revolutionize miniature drone technology and I can't take that kind of time away from it. I don't go in much for being pampered anyway, it's boring." She grinned. "I get enough pampering here at home." She had recently developed an interest in Jared Smoot, the rangy, whipcord thin reconnaissance specialist and highly skilled sniper of Team Dallas. Fly wasn't the least bit shy.

# Chapter Three

**Ko Phai Isand, Bay of Bangkok, one year ago.**

Bykov was a brutally handsome man by any standards and he knew it. As host at Pleasures he planned to regularly hold small, intimate dinner parties and soirees. The guests invited would feel singled out as special, somehow superior or more elite than the other guests—and that was precisely what he intended. It was at these functions that he personally would evaluate the suitability of the candidates Orel singled out for his ransom scheme.

"That one has spirit, and she has the look. I think we should invite her to dine with me this evening, Mikhail. See to it, will you?" It was not a request but an order.

"The blonde as well?" Mikhail did not even glance up from his laptop. He knew precisely who Bykov was referring to—Emily Larroquette. The blonde, Mimi Cardone, of the Miami Cardones, was always within earshot of the Larroquette woman as was at least one of the dangerously beautiful South African bodyguards. Mikhail did not even bother to ask about the bodyguards. He would arrange for some way to have them fed in the kitchen. The society women would never appreciate having the hired help sitting at table with them as if they were equals.

"Pick several more of the loveliest and invite them to dine with me, Mikhail, but make sure the Larroquette woman is seated next to me … and her blonde friend at the other end of the table." The easiest way to charm one of these women was to sit her among strangers instead of among friends. That way, with his personal attributes, some of the finest food and wine, and a little judicious flattery, Bykov would be able to get them to focus on him alone. The tactics had worked for him in Russia, on the French Riviera, and in Rome; he had every confidence that they would work just as well, if not better, in his own private resort.

One of Mikhail Orel's primary duties at Pleasures was compiling a detailed dossier on the wealthiest and most beautiful of the visitors to the resort. He did a brief background check of all the guests, but the cream garnered most of his attention. If the word "billion" did not pop up in the first cursory online check, he went on to the next guest. Ordinary millionaires were not worthy of his focus or Bykov's attention ... the exceptions being guests of extraordinary beauty. He knew Bykov's tastes.

Bykov's looks, his accent, his European manners, his impeccable Bond Street clothing (all hand tailored) and, of course, his money virtually guaranteed that he would receive many offers from potential bedmates. As a rule, he politely turned them down, careful not to offend them. When he deemed it necessary, he had Mikhail send one of the studs from the poolside wait staff to dance attendance on the disappointed females as a consolation. The waiters and masseurs were the only males allowed at Pleasures other than Bykov and Orel. There were also a smattering of masseuses for those guests so inclined. Even the maintenance staff was comprised of females.

It was his policy that he would never take a guest to his bedchamber at Pleasures, no matter how sorely he was tempted. When he felt the need badly enough, Bykov would fly a highly accomplished courtesan from Bangkok to Logovo for his pleasure. He was building a sterling reputation for the ultimate in security and safety for his guests, and as a result he'd developed a clientele consisting of only the ladies of the ultra-rich. The easier they were to convince of their own uniqueness the more likely he believed his demands for immediate, discreet payment would be satisfied—and with no complications from the international law enforcement community.

* * *

The private dining room featured a magnificent table constructed of four-inch slabs of Birdseye maple and polished to a fine sheen only with natural oils. The exquisite china and silver had been in Bykov's family for generations and bore his family crest. He had managed to spirit it out of the estate in St. Petersburg at enormous expense when he had terminated his association with the Russian Mafia. It had not been an easy task. There were twelve matching chairs, six to a side, and one at the head of the table that had been carved to look like a wooden throne by a serf from the estate in the early 1700s.

Bykov, resplendent in white tie and tails, sat at the head of the table with Emily Larroquette to his right. Two bottles of 2006 Lafite-Rothschild Bordeaux sat on a crisp doily before him, breathing. A delicate, exquisitely beautiful trio of Thai women entered the dining room bearing plates with the first course of dinner—a walnut, arugula and gorgonzola crostini—quickly followed by courses of baby artichokes with a zesty mustard dipping sauce, fresh garden salad with mushroom stuffed salmon lox balls, and julienne snow peas and carrots. Before each course, the trio would remove the empty plates before bringing in the next course on fresh, gleaming china. For the fifth course, a female chef entered the dining area with a standing rib roast of beef and carved it on the table and slid it onto fresh china plates, which were then delivered to the guests by the trio. It was an elegant and impressive display. The final course was a chocolate concoction created by the chef exclusively for Pleasures.

Even the most cultured and refined women at the table were impressed by the food, the atmosphere, and the service, and Bykov beamed at them all from his wooden throne while amusing the ladies with anecdotes about his life in Mother Russia. The conversation around the table was light and lively. Emily's bodyguards were served, one at a time, in the kitchen. The one not eating at the time stood watch behind Emily's chair while the other guests pretended not to notice.

All the guests were generally qualified, as only the truly wealthy could afford the prices he charged for a stay at Pleasures. A further qualification was physical beauty, though that was a matter of personal choice as opposed to a financial consideration. Bykov's private apartment at Logovo could accommodate up to six women ... a personal harem. As a former Polkovnic of the SVR, he was intimately familiar with the techniques, methods and procedures used to condition human minds.

One of the projects he had supervised had been a detailed study of how to go about effectively cultivating the Stockholm Syndrome in test subjects. The results had surpassed all his expectations, but he had concealed them from his superiors in the SVR. He had falsified the reports he turned in, the glimmer of an idea about how he could personally profit from the program already beginning to form in the back of his mind. It had been risky to subvert the program and deceive the SVR, but it was about to pay off in a major way. The illicit money he had made as a Russian Mafia don was a pittance compared to the prospective income from the ransom scheme. He also believed it would be a far less hazardous venture personally; his capture and renovation of the remote vastness of Logovo, his private cadre of 'cultural aides', and an immensely expensive helicopter were assurance of that. Only when he had the apparatus for the implementation of his scheme in place would he risk taking one of the guests to Logovo for his personal pleasure.

Bykov had resolved the problem of distance between Pleasures, Logovo, Bangkok, and the widely dispersed areas where he would complete the repatriation of his abductees with the hijacking of an Airbus twin-turbine rotorcraft. The helicopter had a maximum speed of 175 knots, or

201 miles per hour. The H225 (previously designated as a Eurocopter EC225 Super Puma) was a long-range passenger transport helicopter developed by Eurocopter as the next generation of the civilian Super Puma family. It could carry up to 24 passengers along with two crew and a cabin attendant, depending on how the buyer wanted it configured.

Formerly the property of a minor African potentate, who had merely shrugged and ordered a new one believing the previous one had been stolen by a neighboring petty tyrant, the aircraft was fitted with state-of-the-art avionics and autopilot systems that had been proven across the Super Puma family. Two powerful Turbomeca Makila 2A engines, a stout five-bladed main rotor and a Spheriflex rotor head gave the H225 a fantastic range, fast cruising speed, and a flight endurance of about 5 hours and 38 minutes. Extravagant and impressive, the helicopter was perfect for his needs.

*Track Down Thailand*

\* \* \*

## Rifle range, Brad's ranchette, present day.

"The lack of recoil in this thing never ceases to amaze me, Vicky."

Brad was referring to the AA-12, a full automatic 12-gauge shotgun with a relatively low cyclic rate of 300 rounds per minute permitting the shooter to fire one round at a time with brief trigger pulls. The weapon can be fed by either an 8-shell box magazine, or a 20- or 32-shell drum magazine. He ejected the empty 32-round magazine and shoved a full 8-round magazine into the magazine well before handing it to Vicky.

Vicky, an expert with firearms in her own right, took the shotgun, getting a feel for the stubby, futuristic weapon before lifting it up to her shoulder. A row of watermelons rested on a fence twenty yards down the range Brad had constructed well away from the house and outbuildings so as not to disturb Ving's kids or the animals he was planning to purchase as soon as he could find the time. Vicky tickled the trigger of the shotgun, setting off two rounds. She made a mental note that she would be able to let off a single round fairly easily once she got used to the trigger pull. Then she depressed the trigger and emptied the magazine.

"That's amazing," she said, holding her hand out for one of the larger drum magazines. Brad handed her one and she snapped it into place, chambered a round and emptied it in short three-round bursts.

"This thing would be murder in a close-quarters firefight."

"Yeah it would," Brad said, reaching for the still smoking weapon. "I'm just afraid the same thing that makes it so deadly for bad guys will put hostages at risk. This thing will clear a room in the blink of an eye, but target discrimination is going to be a problem." He snapped in another 32-round drum and experimented with one, two, and three-round bursts, adjusting his trigger pull and getting a feel for the futuristic shotgun. "It does have its uses though, baby. I can see where it might have some definite advantages over those American 180s we have."

The American-180 is a submachine gun developed in the 1960s, which fires .22 LR cartridges from a 225 round pan magazine and a cyclic rate of fire of 1200 rounds per minute. The relatively weak .22 cal rounds were devastating when they poured from the barrel of the weapon, and they made a sound that was like that of the world's largest hive of pissed-off bumblebees.

He set the shotgun down on the range table and opened the Hoppes cleaning kit.

"Have you given any more thought to Willona's suggestion yet?"

"About that fancy resort?"

"Yes."

"Brad, that place is halfway around the world and it's probably way overpriced. I want a vacation, but I can stay somewhere a lot closer to Dallas for a hell of a lot less money."

Brad dropped his cleaning rod and pulled Vicky into his arms.

"Vicky, baby, you've been through a lot with us. You've been hurt, you've come through like a real badass when we needed you. You want a girly vacation; I want you to have the best. The money is not an issue, we've got more now than I ever thought we'd have. Why don't you go ahead and have a talk with Jess about it?"

Vicky wrapped her arms around his neck and kissed him.

"Did I ever tell you that you're sweet?"

"No," he growled, "and don't you go telling anybody else that either. I've got a reputation to uphold."

"Ooorah!" she whispered as she kissed him again.

* * *

"You two ought to go to that resort, Vicky, from what Willona told me, the guest list is a who's who of the ultra-rich and famous."

"That's what I've been telling her," Jessica said enthusiastically. "I've been to the website and it looks fabulous!"

"I told you, Fly, I can get almost as good somewhere closer to Dallas for a lot less money … and I have absolutely no interest in hanging out with a bunch of vapid jet-setters that I have nothing in common with."

"You haven't even looked at the website, Vicky. The place is totally gorgeous and it caters only to women."

"Just what I need, to be surrounded by women who love to name drop and be the center of attention."

"Oh, it's a lot more than that, Vicky. They have sailing, scuba diving, snorkeling, deep sea fishing charters … and one of the masseurs is a two-time Mr. Universe!"

Vicky's eyes showed a spark of interest for the first time. She was pretty sure that her relationship with Brad was going to eventually turn into something permanent, but the idea of being manhandled by a gorgeous hunk of man was not without its charm…

"Maybe someday, Jess, let me think about it a little."

Jessica Paul smiled, a soft, secret smile. Vicky was hooked and she knew it. It was just a matter of time and a few gentle nudges here and there. She made a mental note to check and see if her passport needed renewal.

# Chapter Four

**Ko Phai Island, Bay of Bangkok, present day.**

"Welcome once again, Miss Larroquette! It's been too long."

The front desk was nothing like front desks in other resorts. The exotically beautiful Thai woman, Mai, who received all the guests, did so in an elegantly appointed sitting room just inside the main entrance. An antique Russian tea set, comprised of a samovar, a teapot, a sugar pot with a spoon and two jugs, one smaller and one larger, graced a Russian Imperial style Dore bronze malachite table. Each piece featured Bykov's engraved family crest and a crown on their bodies.

Emily Larroquette's imminent arrival had prompted Mai to have Jasmine green tea imported from China, Emily's favorite, poured into the freshly washed samovar and kept at exactly 90 degrees. Jasmine flowers were placed around the tea tray that the samovar sat upon.

Mai filled a small, delicate Wu Shuang Pu handleless porcelain teacup from the Tongzhi period, the porcelain so thin that it was nearly transparent, with the fragrant tea and presented it to Emily with both hands, her head bowed respectfully.

Accepting Mai's deference as only her due, Emily took the cup and politely took a tiny sip. Lifting her lips from the cup, she made a moue of distaste.

"Mai, really! You know I always take two lumps of sugar in my tea."

Mai managed to suppress the irritation she felt at Emily's rudeness. She had put two cubes of sugar in the cup before she'd poured the tea from the silver teapot, and she'd even stirred it while Emily watched the little ritual.

"Certainly Miss Emily, my apologies, I can't imagine what I was thinking." She lifted another cube from the sugar bowl with a pair of silver tongs. Her movements were studied and graceful. With exaggerated delicacy, she stirred the brew in the cup and again presented it to Emily, who made another face when she sipped again. The Jasmine tea was no longer the correct temperature, precisely 90 degrees, but she was willing to be magnanimous about it.

"Why thank you, Mai, that was delicious!"

Mai then gave Emily the electronic key card to her favorite suite and bowed deeply from the waist, her displeasure masked by the false smile on her face. Mai was very good at her job. When Emily had left and Mai was certain she was alone, she stepped between the security camera that Bykov and Orel did not know she was aware of and the samovar. Surreptitiously, she lifted the lid of the samovar and spit into the jasmine tea. When she replaced the lid, her smile was genuine. After a few moments savoring what she had done, she pressed the buzzer cleverly hidden beneath the coffee table and another Thai woman wearing a crimson cheongsam with a dragon embroidered on it in gold thread came to take the samovar away and wash it. The enigmatic smile on her face said she knew exactly what Mai had done. Emily Larroquette was not popular with the Pleasures staff.

* * *

The suite had a very familiar feel to it when Emily Larroquette stepped inside. Her luggage, of course, had been brought to her suite and unpacked, her clothing arranged and put away, and the luggage itself carted off to storage. Everything was right where Emily expected it to be. It was her third visit to the exclusive resort, each stay longer than the one before. This time she had booked the suite for a month-long stay, but that was okay. Daddy was paying for it to make up for the fact that he was taking his latest girlfriend with him to Paris instead of taking Emily as he had promised. She didn't mind. The only thing she liked about that dirty city was the shopping.

Sighing with pleasure, she stepped into her dressing room, where a pleasant surprise awaited her. The full length mirror that had been inside on her first three visits had been replaced by a gilt-framed full-length tri-fold mirror. Eagerly she stripped off the Alexandre Vauthier draped jersey deep-v ruched dress and dropped it to the floor carelessly, as if the two-thousand-dollar garment was a pair of cheap jeans or a tee shirt. The maid staff would pick it up later. In short order her panties and bra joined the high-dollar pile on the floor. Emily stood in front of the new mirror nude and examined her body with a critical eye.

A tawny mane of sun-streaked hair cascaded in a cloud down past her shoulders in back, and down to the soft curves of her breasts in front. The soft cloud of hair framed wide-set hazel eyes over aristocratic cheekbones, an exquisitely formed nose, and a wide, generous mouth with pouty lips. The skin of her slender neck was smooth and unlined. When her eyes dropped again to her perfectly shaped breasts, she loved to note that there were no tan lines there. All of her skin had a creamy golden tan that was one of the few things she actually worked at to maintain.

Her firm, flat belly, narrow waist, the gentle swell of her hips, and long shapely legs had to be the result of extraordinary genes because Emily was no athlete and she hated working out. Well into her thirties, she had somehow managed to avoid the ravages of the dissolute life she'd led. Pleased with what she saw, she took the tiniest Italian string bikini she'd ever purchased from its package, contemplated it for mere seconds before tossing the top to the floor where her dress and undergarments lay puddled in a heap. Slipping into the almost non-existent garment she then collected the fresh monogrammed white robe provided by Pleasures from the foot of the bed where the maid had left it. Careful not to appear too eager, she hurried out to the pool area. From there, after taking a drink or two by the pool, she would go to the place she was itching to go and the real reason she'd been so anxious to get to Pleasures this time. Jason.

As she settled into her favorite chaise lounge, the one in Jason's area, she covertly scanned the modest crowd for his spectacular physique. She had a moment's anxiety when she didn't spot him right away, but she breathed a sigh of relief when he suddenly appeared from one of the cabanas. Then she experienced a brief flash of irritation when a startlingly beautiful and extremely skimpily dressed young woman followed him out of the cabana. The irritation dissipated almost immediately when a slightly older woman appeared in the door of the cabana and summoned the diminutive girl back.

Stepping back just inside the doorway, the woman drew the girl into a heated embrace, followed by a passionate goodbye kiss. Emily felt the heat already building in her belly flare up intensely. So Jason and the girl worked in tandem? How curious! How fascinating…

\* \* \*

Seated at his desk, his customary spot in the heat of the afternoon, Bykov scrolled through the surveillance cameras until he found the one he wanted—one of the private massage rooms in the spa. He tapped the wireless mouse once and the high-resolution image expanded to full screen size. Emily Larroquette was lying naked on the massage table, totally engrossed in the attentions of Jason and Chloe together.

*Fascinating! I never would have expected that, though given her proclivities I should have figured it out before now.*

"Mikhail?"

"Yes sir?"

"Is there anything in your dossier on Ms. Larroquette that indicates she has ever had more than a passing interest in an amorous relationship with a member of her own gender?"

Orel glanced up in surprise.

"No sir. I'd have remembered something like that."

Bykov grunted and turned his attention back to the monitor in front of him. It wasn't like Mikhail to miss something like this. Ms. Larroquette must be expanding her horizons.

*Interesting! She's definitely matured into a true beauty over the last year, and she certainly has no inhibitions … judging from what I can see here. Perhaps…*

"Mikhail!"

"Yes sir?" Something in Bykov's tone made him sit up alertly.

"I want you to find me something juicy on Clarence Larroquette, something I can use to influence him."

Orel considered the order for a moment. Bykov obviously wanted dirt on the Larroquette man, and that set Orel's mind to working furiously. His instant conclusion was that his boss had decided to finally activate the revenue stream that the Pleasures venture had been created to generate.

"Yes sir!"

"And Mikhail?"

"Yes sir?"

"I need that as soon as possible." Bykov turned his attention back to the graphic display of raw lust on the monitor in front of him.

\* \* \*

Bykov studied the flimsy in his hands with an amused expression on his face. Mikhail had been careful not to make an electronic record of this investigation, and this hand-typed flimsy was the only copy in existence. This evidence was dynamite, but it would be of no value to Bykov should it become known to anyone else. Mikhail was very good at his job, and he had immediately recognized the value of this information.

*At last! It's time to implement the plan I have worked so long to bring about, spent so much of my resources on. Once Larroquette is aware that I have this information he will pay whatever I demand, and he will do so without question—and without notifying the authorities!*

Uncharacteristically, he allowed his mind to wander for a bit. *Who would have guessed she would have gone this far overboard and so quickly? She's been enamored of Jason since her first stay here and she's made use of him every time ... but not the way she has Chloe. Those two she-bulldogs of hers have never even allowed anyone else in her suite before, not even Miss Cardone, her bosom friend. They are decidedly unhappy that Chloe has been spending every night in there with her during this stay. This appears to be a new quirk, and it seems as if she can't get enough. Between this and her father's iniquities, I should have enough leverage not only to profit from this but perhaps to indulge in some guilty pleasures of my own!*

Bykov saved then reversed the surveillance footage from the massage salon and watched intently as the three figures on the monitor engaged in a most delightful and almost gymnastic ménage à trois. He felt himself stir and surreptitiously put his hand in his lap.

*Scott Conrad*

\* \* \*

Dressed in white tie and tails, Bykov sat in his private dining room, where no guest had ever been before, sipping his favorite aperitif, Campari on the rocks. A silver candelabra graced the center of the polished mahogany table, the flickering flames of the slender white candles casting dancing shadows on the pristine white walls. His personal china, stemware, and silverware were set artfully for an intimate dinner for two. The soft strains of a classical piece by Vivaldi or Mozart, Bykov could never remember which, were wafting through the air, barely audible, as a mood setter.

Emily had been flattered to receive the engraved invitation to dine alone with Bykov, and she had deliberately chosen the most revealing, provocative Balmain evening dress in her collection to wear for the occasion. The neckline of the form-fitting garment was open to the navel in front, exposing the half globes of her breasts, and the skirt was slit all the way up to her hip. She wore nothing underneath.

She felt his eyes on her the moment she was ushered into the room, and her movements automatically became more sinuous, more feline. Bykov stood when she entered and stepped forward to greet her. Emily turned first one cheek then the other toward the distinguished looking owner of Pleasures, expecting the normal "air" kiss exchanged between members of the jet set. Instead, she felt his hands on her bare shoulders and his lips brushing her ears. Before he let her go, he stared directly into her eyes and then unabashedly dropped his eyes to the deep cut of her décolletage and then lingered on her breasts. Emily felt her nipples harden beneath the thin jersey fabric of the dress until they were standing out conspicuously. Rather than attempt to cover up, she threw her shoulders back proudly and gave him a defiant smile, daring him to continue staring. Unperturbed, Bykov took both her hands and spread them apart. Then his eyes traveled the length of her body from shoulders to toes.

A thrill coursed through Emily's body and she shivered with pleasure as he devoured her with his eyes. Her own eyes fluttered with wanton pleasure. She fed on the lustful looks of men the way a vampire would feed on blood.

"My dear Ms. Larroquette, you do look lovely tonight." He bowed at the waist and kissed the top of her right hand. "I'm so pleased that you decided to accept my invitation."

"I assure you, Mr. Bykov, the pleasure is all mine." She glanced around approvingly at the arrangements he had made and then smiled demurely. "Thank you, this is quite lovely. You've gone to a lot of trouble to make everything absolutely perfect."

"And I can assure you, Miss Larroquette, the pleasure is all mine." He stepped away from her and slid the chair closest to his own back far enough away from the table that she could sit down and then gestured with his hand for her to do so. He hovered above and behind her and she felt rather than noticed his eyes peering down into her décolletage as she hunched her shoulders forward slightly, causing the soft material to open even further, giving him an unobstructed view. She was slightly miffed when Bykov didn't seem to notice. Instead, he pushed her chair in closer to the table and then took his own seat beside her.

He reached for the open bottle of wine with one broad hand and lifted her wine goblet with the other. With unexpected grace he filled the goblet half full and then lifted it to his lips, taking a tiny sip before handing it to her.

Emily took the goblet, licked her lips lasciviously, and took a mouthful of the wine, swishing it around. Her eyebrows rose high on her forehead as she set the goblet down and reached for the bottle. The label read, "Château Mouton Rothschild Pauillac Red Bordeaux, Blend 1945."

"I'm impressed, Mr. Bykov. My father is something of a connoisseur, and I've tasted this before." Her father had indeed been fortunate enough to find a bottle of the particularly rare vintage on an online auction list. Emily had never seen Clarence Larroquette so excited, and she had flown with him to Sotheby's, London, on New Bond Street, Mayfair, to bid on the single bottle available there. Larroquette had been the highest bidder ... he'd paid thirty-three thousand dollars to take it home. He had invited several of his friends, wine aficionados all, to a dinner party, where they only expected to touch and inspect the rare prize. To their consternation, he had actually opened the bottle and shared it with them. Emily, seventeen at the time, had been permitted her own tiny wine glass.

The smile Bykov flashed her was one of genuine pleasure. His estimation of her went up a notch. Perhaps Emily Larroquette was a bit more refined than he had assumed.

He poured more of the wine into her glass and then filled his own three quarters full before setting the bottle back down on the antique Russian silver salver it had been sitting on.

"I'm pleased that you can appreciate a great wine, Miss Larroquette …"

Emily reached out with one shapely, graceful hand, extending her forefinger to stroke the top of Bykov's hand suggestively.

"Oh please, Mr, Bykov, call me Emily."

"Then you must call me Kirill."

"Of course, Kirill." She let her hand linger for a moment before withdrawing it.

Bykov studied her for mere seconds before coming to a decision.

"Miss Emily, would it be forward if I invited you to take a ride in my helicopter after we have our dinner? I think I would enjoy showing you the lights of Bangkok by night."

Emily laughed delightedly.

"I'd love it! I adore riding in Daddy's helicopter at home."

Bykov tapped a concealed button beneath the table with his forefinger and smiled graciously at his guest. Everything was going as he had planned.

\* \* \*

Mikhail, awaiting the signal in the kitchen beside the chef, carefully emptied the contents of a glassine envelope into a snifter of Louis XIII Cognac. The powder would take effect within the hour, and Emily Larroquette would lose whatever inhibitions she had. She would also lose any memory of what transpired when the effects of the drug wore off. Mikhail smiled. His boss was in for an interesting evening.

The Tai chef watched out of the corner of his eye, pretending not to notice. He spoke no English at all, but he knew what he was seeing. He had seen it often enough in the bars and restaurants of Bangkok. It amused him that these American women had to be drugged to do what any sane bar girl would do in Bangkok at the drop of a hat for a man like Bykov—a man with money to burn. Ridiculous!

# Chapter Five

**Rifle range, Brad's ranchette, present day.**

"Be careful with these little beggars," Fly was saying. "These miniature drones are cross stabilized in flight, but when they are resting on this table, a good gust of wind will blow them completely away—and we will never find them." On a white linen tablecloth draped over the firing range table lay four miniature drones that resembled tiny mosquito robots. A thin gauzy fabric with Velcro along the edges was holding the micro drones down, keeping the wind from sweeping them away.

"I can barely see them damn things," Ving was muttering as he peered down at the minuscule objects on the table.

Brad glanced over at his massive friend. The hot Texas sun reflected off Ving's bald pate blindingly.

Ving's skin was so black that it almost appeared blue, and he was sweating fiercely in the heat.

"I'm pretty sure that's the whole idea, Ving. If they were any bigger people could spot them."

"I think they're just darling!" Jessica, dressed in a halter top, low-riding denim cutoffs, and sandals, was totally taken with Fly's gadget wizardry and bent down so close to the gauzy fabric that her nose almost touched it.

"None of you has ever seen one of these, got it?" Fly was in instructor mode and no one wanted to interrupt her, so they all simply nodded their heads in assent. She continued in the same professorial tone. "They were my idea, of course, but Rankin over in DARPA at Fort Meade was developing them for me."

DARPA (Defense Advanced Research Projects Agency) is the agency of the United States DoD responsible for developing emerging technologies for use by the military. DARPA comes up with and creates research and development projects that form the cutting edge of technology and science, many times far exceeding immediate U.S. military requirements.

"I took them with me when I left. Rankin was not very happy with me, but that's his problem. I've been working on them in my spare time at home. I've still got some bugs, pun intended, to work out, but I'm waiting to do those until you finish that nice hermetically sealed lab for me in the barn."

Brad had promised the research lab as part of his inducement for Fly to come to work for him, and he had spent a fortune on lab equipment, much of which had not been delivered yet. Construction of the 5000-square-foot facility was complete, to include the specially constructed environmental control system, but the delivery date on some of the more exotic lab equipment was still a couple of months off.

"How much noise do those gadgets make?" Vicky was intrigued by the possibilities presented by the tiny drones, but she did not see how they could avoid attracting attention in a very quiet environment.

"A great deal of thought and effort went into the construction of the airfoils on these drones. The noise they make flying is almost undetectable by the human ear. The real advantage, however, is that most of the drone is made of ABS plastic and optic fibers. Only the most sensitive of detection devices can recognize one of these as a bug. You can fly one of these suckers and land it on a trouser's cuff or a collar and your surveillance subject would be able to carry it into just about anywhere without anyone detecting a bug on him."

"Dayum!" Ving was genuinely impressed.

After Jared Smoot, Ving could move more quietly than any other member of Team Dallas. Jared was a virtual ghost. Brad had once seen Jared get so close to a hostile sitting by a campfire that he could literally reach out and touch the man's boots without ever being seen. The enormous potential in these tiny flying objects would vastly increase all of their abilities to gather vital intelligence without being detected.

Jessica stepped back from the table so Charlie and Pete could get a closer look at Fly's newest toys. As she stepped back, Brad noticed that his beautiful cousin was still limping slightly from the bad parachute landing she'd made in Wyoming. The jump had been a difficult one, at night by the dark of the moon, carrying a heavily loaded equipment bag, onto a rock-filled DZ. The landing had not been an error at all, what had happened to Jessica could have happened to any of them. Even so, Brad could not resist a sly dig at his cousin.

"Maybe we should consider some remedial PLF training, huh Jess?" A PLF is a parachute landing fall taught to all beginning jumpers using a standard parachute. Jessica had jumped a RAM air parachute, a highly steerable rectangular-shaped chute, capable of a very large glide range, comprised of several tubular panels sewed together. Landing was accomplished by steering into the wind and pulling down hard on the rear toggles. Reasonably adept jumpers managed to land lightly on two feet with little or no jolt whatsoever. Landing with a standard parachute, the landing jolt was equivalent to the one a normal person would feel jumping from the roof of a one-story house. PLF's enabled the body to absorb that jolt with the motion similar to that used by tossing a pitchfork of hay over one's shoulder and rolling onto the ground rather than landing stiff legged.

"Yeah! Maybe you should go back to ground school…" Ving flashed a wicked grin at the svelte blonde beauty.

"Stick it where the sun don't shine, Ving," Jessica retorted. She was irked by the teasing but not really mad.

"People," Fly called out impatiently. "If I'm boring you I'll just take these drones back to my lab. I have plenty of work that I need to get done there!"

"Take it easy, Fly, we're just ribbing her a little."

"I know, Brad. I'm just feeling a little impatient and I'd like them to get in a little practice time flying these. They're very sensitive and they take some getting used to. They're small and they're damned expensive, even for your deep pockets."

Jared Smoot elbowed his way between Charlie and Pete to get a closer look at the drones on the table.

"You sure these things will fly?" His face showed that he was not sure he believed they would. He should have known better than to challenge Fly. The two of them had become something of an item since Fly's introduction to the group. None of them knew for sure, but most of them suspected the budding relationship had involved several sleepovers.

Carefully lifting one corner of the covering gauze, Fly lifted one of the drones with a pair of rubber-tipped tweezers and deposited it in the bottom of a small tumbler. Then she handed Jared an object resembling a slim cell phone.

"This is your flight control. It's simple enough that even you can understand it, Jared." She thrust it into his hands and stepped back, her arms folded across her chest. For just an instant, the look she gave him would have curdled milk.

With a sheepish look on his face, Jared thumbed the power button on and instantly the controls appeared on the touch screen.

"The drone is live now. You can see something that looks like a plus sign with arrow tips at the end of each point inside a double-ringed circle. Using your thumb, you can control the direction of movement by rotating your thumb around the double ring. Up, down, left, right, and all points in between control the direction of flight. The reason I wanted to test this out here in the open is so that you clumsy people don't fly these expensive drones into anything and turn them into high-dollar trash. Think you can handle that, funny boy?"

Chagrined but determined, Jared pushed the up arrow inside the circle. The response of the mosquito-shaped drone was instantaneous. It shot straight up out of the tumbler and almost out of sight before Jared brought it back to level flight.

"How can I tell where it's at if I can't see it?" He stared at the sky blankly.

"Turn on the camera button, Jared."

"You didn't tell me that!" Jared quickly found the second button and pressed it. The entire screen of the control displayed a very clear image, and the flight controls were superimposed on the image.

"As you can see, you control the angle of the camera by controlling the attitude of the drone. It's very simple, but it's highly sensitive. I'm working on buffering that effect, but it's hard to reach an equilibrium between emergency evasive responses and the fine control needed to operate in close quarters."

"How close are you to resolving that issue, Fly?" Brad asked the question more to settle the tension between them than to get an answer.

Fly turned and gave the rugged-looking Team Dallas leader a shrewd look.

"Damned close, Brad, it's just a matter of refining the software and manipulating the buss speed of the propulsion control. Unfortunately, the instrument I need to make that adjustment is still on backorder. As soon as I get it, it will only take a day or so."

Fly turned back to peer around Jared's broad shoulders at the screen of the flight controller.

"You see how the picture is rocking back and forth?" Totally focused on the screen, Jared nodded his head in the affirmative. "There's a tiny blue button on the bottom right corner of the screen. That is a gyroscopic stabilizer. Anytime you're getting the rocking motion on the screen, it means that crosswinds are affecting your flight attitude. Press and hold the blue button until the picture stops rocking and then let go of it." Jared did as he was told and the picture became steady again. He very carefully rotated the drone around until he could see himself and fly on the screen and then brought the drone slowly back to the table. For several tense moments he battled crosswinds and the control sensitivity as he tried to land the drone at the bottom of the tumbler without touching the sides. Finally, the tiny metallic-looking mosquito settled at the bottom of the tumbler and Jared heaved a sigh of relief. His mouth shut in a thin tight line, he handed the flight controller back to Fly.

In an attempt to curb any more friction between the two, Vicky stepped forward and took the control from Fly's hands. Each team member took a turn, and despite Fly's misgivings, they were all able to control the drone through a short flight and land it in the base of the tumbler.

"Do all four of these have the same flight response?"

"They do for the most part, Brad, but there are some subtle differences. That's the reason I brought one of each type out here for everybody to fly."

Each team member took a turn with the remaining three variations of the drone as Fly explained the purposes of the variations in type.

When they were finished, Fly carefully lifted each drone and set it in its own padded container. Gathering them up and setting them in a slim briefcase, Fly, still a little miffed with Jared, walked away from the team toward the barn and her incomplete lab.

"Man, I think you better get to steppin' if you don't wanna miss out on your lovin' tonight." Ving was sincere, but it was funny and the rest of the team suppressed grins as Jared turned to follow the tiny woman.

\* \* \*

Jessica was sitting on one of the lawn chairs on Brad's back patio reading a glossy brochure intently. The rest of the team was engaged in an animated discussion about Fly's new gadgets.

Vicky glanced up and noticed the look of concentration on Jess's face and got up to drag another lawn chair over beside the younger woman.

"Why aren't you in on this conversation, girl? You'll be using these things too, you know."

Jessica didn't look up from her brochure, but she did respond.

"Fly will always have some new thingamajig for us to play with, and I know I'll be getting plenty of training on them when she gets all the glitches out of them."

"So what's got you so serious?" Vicky asked, batting playfully at the high gloss brochure in Jess's lap.

Jessica finally looked up at the woman she had come to trust with her life and grinned.

"I sent off for this just for a few laughs after Willona mentioned the place. You've just got to see it for yourself, Vicky!"

"What is it?"

"It's this place, this Khwām S̄uk̄h. It's absolutely unbelievable! It's for women only and, believe me, it's got everything a girl needs to keep her content."

"I find that hard to believe, Jess. For starters, I can't imagine staying some place where there aren't any men ... that would bore me to tears."

"That's what I thought too," Jessica said with a smug grin. "But wait 'til you get a load of this place!" She handed the brochure to Vicky and leaned back in her chair to watch Vicky's face as she flipped through the thick pages.

The first page showed an opulent bedroom, magnificently furnished with what looked like genuine antiques—very feminine, like something Marie Antoinette would have slept in. The Italian marble bathrooms had gold fixtures and were the size of small apartments. The second and third pages showed various suites available, just as elegantly appointed. Very nice, but nothing that really made an impression on her. The next few pages showed an elegant restaurant and some interesting boutiques with some easily recognizable haute couture house names from Italy and France. That piqued Vicky's interest but only mildly. There were three pages devoted to activities offered at the resort, all included in the monstrously high all-inclusive rate. The final pages, however, caused her eyes to widen appreciatively and her eyebrows to crawl so high on her forehead that one looked like a stylized question mark.

"Pretty hot, huh?"

"I thought you said this place was for women only."

"I didn't say there were no men there, Vicky, I said it's for women only."

"What are you two all fired up about?"

Vicky looked up to see Brad towering over her and she instinctively closed the brochure. The instant she did so she felt foolish. She and Brad had never discussed the status of their relationship, they had merely enjoyed it. There had been no pledge, no commitment to monogamy, and, besides, all she had been doing was looking at a photo of a man ... a Greek god of a man, yes, in tiny abbreviated shorts and nothing else, but still just a man.

"We were looking at a picture of one of the masseurs at Khwām Šukh," she said archly, "see?" She opened the brochure back to the page she had been looking at for Brad to see. "Apparently some men are allowed there after all."

"But he's not a guest, right?"

"No Brad, he's a staff member," Jessica interjected quickly. She had never known Brad to be the jealous type, but she wanted to go to the resort and she didn't want anything to crop up that would spoil her chances. It was going to be hard enough to convince Charlie that it was okay for her to go. If Vicky wouldn't go with her, she'd have no chance at all.

Brad bent down and kissed Vicky on the cheek.

"It looks like a great place, baby, why don't you go ahead? Stay a week or two and get rested up some."

Vicky and Jessica both stared after him open-mouthed as he sauntered over to the cooler and brought out two more Lone Stars for himself and Ving.

"I'm pretty sure I'm going to get pretty attached to the one that looks like a little metallic mosquito, guys." The brochure and the masseur with the movie star looks were already out of his mind.

# Chapter Six

**Los Angeles, California, present day.**

Clarence Larroquette was bone tired. He'd just finished a grueling negotiation in Lagos, Nigeria with a medium-sized independent producer there and had flown back to LAX in his corporate Gulfstream G650. Far from being a luxury craft, despite the fine appointments, the G650 was an airborne, fully staffed office and communications center. Larroquette had worked continuously all the way home. One of the multibillionaire's quirks was that, despite being a wine connoisseur, when he had a taste for brandy, he preferred an ordinary, inexpensive brand of V.S.O.P.

It was only on the limo ride back to his Malibu Beach Colony estate, relaxing for the first time in weeks and sipping on a snifter of his favorite brandy that he realized that he'd not heard from Emily since she had left for that fancy resort in

Thailand. He reached for the cell phone in the breast pocket of his immaculate pinstriped charcoal-gray Brioni three-piece suit and pushed the speed dial number for his personal assistant, Lucas Merriwether. Merriwether had not rated a ride in the limo, having come down with some ridiculous Nigerian bug that had rendered him virtually useless in the recent negotiations, and was currently on his way home to his family in Bel Air in an airport limo.

"Yes sir?" Merriwether's response to Larroquette's call was instantaneous, even though he had a temperature of 102 and felt nauseous.

"Merriwether, have you heard from Emily lately?"

"No sir, but I can check with Sarah and see if she has." Sarah was Larroquette's personal secretary, a stunning blonde California beach bunny and Stanford graduate with a surprisingly brilliant mind who had been more than willing to satisfy Larroquette's baser urges in exchange for a salary in the low six figures and a cushy job with great perks in an exclusive high-rise office building in downtown L.A.

* * *

"Sarah, it's me, Merriwether…"

"Hey Luke, I didn't know you were back!" Her voice dropped a note. "Does he need me out at the beach house?" If her boss required her services she would have to postpone her date with Dan Treadwell down in Maintenance. Dan spent his weekends lifting weights at Venice Beach, preparing for the next Mr. Universe competition. He was not the sharpest pencil in the box, but when she could entice him away from his mirror he was able to give her a spirited workout.

"No, no, nothing like that. He wants to know if you've heard from Emily."

"Well, why doesn't he just call her? I programmed her numbers into his cell phone.

"No Luke, I haven't heard from her since she told me she was booking another stay at Khwām Šukh over in Thailand." She hesitated. "Why? Is something wrong?" She was already thumbing through her contacts on her new iPhone for Annika Pedersen, the senior of the two South African mercenaries Larroquette had hired to be Emily's personal bodyguards. Annika was as deadly as she was hot looking, which was saying something as far as Sarah was concerned.

"The boss was asking—he hasn't heard from her in a while and you know how he is about Emily…"

"Got it Luke, I'm calling Annika now. Want to stay on this line? I'm sure everything's fine." She didn't wait for an answer; she punched in Annika's speed dial number and waited for a second for the overseas number to ring. Annika always answered on the first ring, but not this time. By the second ring Sarah was concerned. By the third ring she was alarmed. Punching the "End Call" button, she quickly pushed the speed dial button for Kaya Hendriks, the other bodyguard, with the same result. She turned back to her desk phone and spoke into the handset.

"Luke? Yes, give me a minute and let me get back to you, okay?" She managed to keep the concern out of her voice, but Luke was well aware how unusual it was for Sarah not to have instant communications with Emily's bodyguards. He was concerned for Emily, of course, but he was more concerned about the delay in responding to Larroquette's demand.

In near panic mode, Sarah reached for her old-fashioned Rolodex and quickly found the card with the number for Khwām Sukh, listed, of course, under Pleasures. Emily had explained to her, in fascinating detail, exactly what was so appealing about the exclusive resort. She'd even showed Sarah pictures, taken on her own diamond-encrusted iPhone. The pictures had been explicit, and they had been of a gorgeous man that made Dan Treadwell look like second-hand goods.

The receptionist at Pleasures was politely insistent that Miss Emily Larroquette and company had checked out of the resort the night before and had left no information as to where she might be going. The panic was real now. Sarah checked with Larroquette's aviation office at LAX to see if Emily had called for transportation as she usually did, but the manager assured her that Miss Emily had certainly not ordered up a flight from Bangkok.

In full panic mode, Sarah quickly checked with all the major airlines out of Bangkok. When they had no information, she began the laborious chore of running down all the private charter jet operators. She was halfway through the list of those when it occurred to her that she was wasting time. Emily always used her father's American Express Centurion card for purchases, she didn't even carry cash.

To Sarah's consternation, the last transaction registered on Emily's card had been the day she arrived at Pleasures. It was a substantial purchase, at least by Sarah's standards, but there had been nothing since. She slowly closed the screen with the charge card information and reached for the landline. She wasn't about to tell Clarence Larroquette that his precious daughter was missing and that no one had the remotest idea where she had gone. That was Luke's job.

\* \* \*

Technically the two South African mercenaries were not his responsibility; they worked directly for and reported directly to Clarence Larroquette. Merriwether considered his options very carefully. Larroquette was an impatient man when it came to his daughter's welfare, but the man would be furious if Merriwether could not personally verify bad news, and this was definitely bad news. Emily had managed to get away from her bodyguards only twice in all the years Merriwether had been working for her father, and both times she had only managed to get away for an hour or two. Larroquette had lashed out at everyone in range, his rage maniacal, and heads had rolled, figuratively speaking. Merriwether had been hired, not because his predecessor had been fired but rather because the man had developed the symptoms of PTSD and had to be hospitalized.

In panic mode, he looked up the numbers Sarah had called and dialed them himself ... with identical results. Then, bracing himself for Larroquette's expected tirade, he called his boss. To his amazement, Clarence Larroquette remained calm and assured Merriwether that he would handle it. Then the phone went dead in his hands.

\* \* \*

Clarence Larroquette punched the "End" button on the call then set his brandy snifter down. He was struggling mightily with his temper. Despite the urgency of the situation, he forced himself to breathe slowly, taking in huge gulps of air. When his rage subsided, he made his limo driver take him on to Malibu.

* * *

Back in his own study, he had the maid prepare his special blend of coffee and bring him a mug. Then he dismissed her and went through a convoluted cigar cutting ritual before lighting the hand-rolled Cuban cigar, rolling it over the flame until there was precisely one half inch of ash before taking a puff. After the first sip of the steaming coffee, he punched the speaker button on his desk phone and waited calmly for Sarah to answer, which she did on the first ring. Larroquette was the only person who had that number.

"Yes sir?" She decided to be formal rather than use her usual flirty tone. He was bound to be upset and she didn't want him to take it out on her.

"Give me the number to that swanky resort."

She did as he asked, the Rolodex still open to the right card, and then the phone went dead. He hadn't sounded angry, but in her experience, that was when he was at his most dangerous. Sarah was glad he'd hung up, and she breathed a sigh of relief as she put the handset back in its cradle.

* * *

"Young lady, do you know who I am?" He was having a hard time reigning in his temper, and the calm, polite voice of the woman who'd identified herself as Mai was almost as infuriating as her denial that she had any idea of Emily's whereabouts or where the two South African bodyguards might be.

"You are Mr. Clarence Harding Larroquette sir, and I know perfectly well who you are—yet I still have no knowledge of where your daughter has gone, please excuse me."

"Let me talk to your manager!"

"As I told you earlier, sir, the manager is not available at this time. So sorry." Mai was unflappable.

Larroquette roared and slammed the phone down hard enough to crack the casing. It took all of five minutes before he was calm enough to send for his chief of security, Michael Harris. Harris, a retired Force Recon Marine, was an impressive specimen. A shade over six feet tall, his rippling musculature showed through his impeccably tailored suit. His blond hair, still cut high and tight in the tradition of the Corps, hid the fact that gray was beginning to invade his temples.

The man moved like a big cat, quickly but without the appearance of hurrying. Despite the fact that he had been awake for more than forty-eight hours, he appeared freshly shaven and his suit still looked as if it had just been pressed. Larroquette often wondered if the man kept a spare suit and a shaving kit handy. He had never seen Harris mussed, not even after he'd subdued three ruffians at Soekarno-Hatta, Jakarta International Airport. The thugs had thought to liberate one of Larroquette's Luis Vuitton suitcases from the luggage carousel. When Harris had politely suggested that they may have picked the wrong suitcase, the men made the mistake of disagreeing with him. Watching the incident unfold convinced Larroquette that he had made the correct decision in hiring the man as his chief of security. The rapid takedown of three hostiles took only seconds, and it was a thing of beauty if one didn't mind the sight of blood.

"Yes sir?"

"Emily is missing, and those damned people at Pleasures or whatever the hell it's called won't tell me anything except that she checked out yesterday and they have no idea where she went."

"Yes sir." He waited for further instructions but not long.

"Get out to LAX. I'll have the G650 refueled and ready by the time you get there."

"Yes sir!" He turned to leave. Larroquette was intensely detail oriented, and he knew that he would receive detailed instructions in flight. The corporate American Express card in his wallet would see to any expenses incurred. Larroquette liked unquestioning obedience.

The G650 was ready, engines running, when Harris arrived at the private terminal at LAX. A fresh crew was on board and they welcomed him aboard without fanfare. As soon as Harris boarded, the door was shut behind him and the sleek bird was rolling. As usual, the Larroquette aircraft was shunted to the head of the takeoff line. Harris had just fastened his seatbelt when he felt the wheels lift off the runway.

*Scott Conrad*

\* \* \*

The flight would be a direct one with a duration of 15 hours 56 minutes, a distance of 8,131 miles. The G650 was fitted with extended range fuel tanks. Harris allowed himself the luxury of a shower, a shave, and a change of suits. He kept five identical suits aboard the aircraft at all times. Mr. Larroquette was fond of neatness, and Harris, a career Marine, had always been fastidious in his dress and grooming.

When he returned from the master suite shower, he removed and hung up his coat and tie before sitting down at Larroquette's desk. The secretary, one of the office staff who had not been changed out at LAX, was startlingly pretty, and she gave Harris a coquettish smile as she handed him a thick dossier fresh from the onboard printer.

Harris acknowledged her with a brief nod of his head as he took the dossier from her hand, but he immediately focused on the contents. There were photographs of the exterior of the resort and of the suites and amenities that apparently had come from brochures, but there was a handwritten note explaining that despite an intensive computer search, there seemed to be no copy of the building plans to be had. There was an aerial photograph, but it just gave the locations of buildings not their functions. The one thing that was clear was that there was only one visible means of entering the walled compound. There was no evidence of security personnel, but there was nothing in the dossier about electronic surveillance of any kind.

Harris allowed himself a hint of a smile. It wasn't as if he were planning a raid or an assault. He was just checking up on the boss's daughter. He thought about Emily Larroquette for a moment and his lips curled into a bigger smile. She was a hellion, that one. She'd once tried to seduce him, back when he'd first come to work for Larroquette. He'd gone to check out the pool area at the Malibu Beach Colony estate, prior to a party the boss was giving. The girl had been lounging beside the pool with her bikini top untied. When she noticed Michael, she had smiled and asked him to come over to where she was sitting. When he'd reached her, she sat up, causing the bikini top to fall, and then licked her lips suggestively and asked him if he'd put some suntan lotion on her back. She had stared brazenly into his eyes while thrusting her small, perfect breasts out at him, daring him not to look. He'd kept his face impassive, but he'd complied with her request. She was a tempting morsel, but she wasn't worth losing this cushy job and all its perks over.

Putting the memory aside, Harris lowered the back of the seat and prepared to nap. It would be a long flight. Plenty of time to catch up on his sleep, and there would be a gourmet meal ready for him when he awakened. He sighed. Michael Harris had loved the Corps, but it had never treated him as well as Clarence Larroquette did.

*Track Down Thailand*

\* \* \*

The sign at the entrance was so discreet that Harris almost missed it. He'd been forced to rent a car because neither of the taxi drivers he'd been able to find would take him there. He'd been forced to use the last of his U.S. currency to even get one of the villagers to give him directions, and that little man had been frightened so badly that he'd insisted on slipping into a narrow alley before he'd talk to Harris—and as soon as he'd whispered the directions, he'd turned and fled as if all the hounds of Hell were after him.

He stopped the car on the side of the road because there was no parking area at all, which Harris thought peculiar, but there was nothing sinister in the appearance of the place. As he approached the gate, he was challenged by a female security guard. Harris had done enough tours in the Far East to recognize a Chinese when he saw one.

"Tíngzhǐ!"

He spoke no Chinese, but he knew from the tone of command in her voice that he had just been commanded to halt.

"I just want to get some information about my boss's daughter, lady, and then I'm out of here."

"Jìnzhǐ! Jìnzhǐ nánrén rùnèi!" (It is forbidden! No men allowed!)

Not intimidated by the slight female, Harris moved forward purposefully. He would gain access to the compound whether she was willing or not. He'd not traveled halfway around the world to be put off by an arrogant Chinese security guard. As he moved closer, a door opened to the side of the guard post, a large door. Out of it stormed half a dozen of the largest Chinese men Harris had ever seen, all taller than him. They didn't speak, they just fell on him.

He could never remember having lost a fight, but he'd never had to fight six men at once before either. He gave a good accounting of himself, but in the end, the Chinese outlasted him. When they were done, a Chinese MengShi 4x4 military jeep came through the garage door opening, and two of the men tossed Harris's torn and bleeding body into the back. He was driven, unconscious, into what passed for a town on Ko Phai Island and dumped unceremoniously into the street. And there he lay until he came to. When he was finally able to move, he noticed a thick manila envelope taped to his ripped and shredded suit jacket. It was addressed to Clarence Harding Larroquette, marked, "Personal, Layla, Eyes Only."

# Chapter Seven

**Los Angeles, California.**

The steward on board the Gulfstream had patched Harris up as best he could, but Harris was limping badly and his face was swollen and bruised when he walked into Larroquette's office. He'd contacted Larroquette the moment he'd gotten aboard the aircraft in Bangkok, his cell phone having been badly damaged in the brawl, before he'd even bothered to clean up. The "Personal, Layla, Eyes Only" marking had given him pause, and he'd waited to ask if he should open it. Larroquette had hesitated a moment and then ordered him not to. Minutes later, the Gulfstream was in the air, and the steward was wondering if he dared put stitches in the cut over Harris's eyebrow. He'd settled on a butterfly bandage and hoped it would hold until they were back in the States.

\* \* \*

Larroquette reached for the manila folder as soon as Harris entered the office.

"Michael, you look like hell. What happened?"

"There were six of them." Harris grimaced. "I could've held my own with three, but there were six of these big bastards. Biggest Chinese I've ever seen." His right arm was in a sling, and there was a bandage across the knuckles of his left hand. With the palm of his left hand, he rubbed his swollen chin gingerly.

"Go see the doctor, Michael, I can take the rest of it from here."

Dismissed, Harris left the office, grateful that he had not received an ass chewing and puzzled because Larroquette had been so calm. He had no intention of going to see a doctor over a few cuts and bruises. There was a very attractive nurse living next door to his apartment in Malibu. On occasion he had asked her to treat minor cuts and bruises and she had been more than sympathetic. She was a great believer in bedrest as a cure all for minor injuries ... and she was good at it.

\* \* \*

With trembling hands, Larroquette broke the seal on the manila folder and slowly withdrew the contents. There, in startling black and white, was photographic evidence that he had indeed fornicated with Layla Robbins, an incredibly attractive female who appeared to be much older than 16 and had a fake ID to prove it. The little bitch had known exactly what she was doing when she came on to him at a little soirée given by her mother, a not so well-to-do socialite from Pasadena. The mother was a distant relative of one of Larroquette's clients in Mumbai. The mother, clever woman that she was, hatched the scheme with her daughter in the hope that they could blackmail him for a substantial sum.

The initial demand had been exorbitant, but Larroquette had negotiated them down to a half million dollars. Even so, a half million dollars was a small enough price to pay to avoid going to prison, not to mention losing billions of dollars in revenue in the process as well as making him a pariah in the social circles where he negotiated his real deals. The mother and daughter had both signed a bogus non-disclosure agreement, apparently unaware that the contract, filled with indecipherable legal mumbo jumbo courtesy of J. Tillsworth Haskins, Esq., the snarky little weasel who was Larroquette's private attorney, was illegal.

Larroquette glanced down at the cover sheet one more time. A hundred million dollars in cash. The money was to be delivered by hand within seven days, and it was to be delivered at sea at coordinates to be given prior to the exchange. The message was clear. There would be no exchange until after the money was received. The message was unsigned, but there was an envelope containing a photo attached. It showed Emily, naked and unconscious, with her hair pulled back and with a wicked-looking knife blade at her neck. He felt as if an ice-cold hand had plunged into his chest and was ripping out his heart when he saw Emily bare and helpless like that.

*I can float the hundred million dollars and have it deposited in any bank in the world with a snap of my fingers, but coming up with a hundred million in cash is an entirely different matter. Nobody keeps that much cash on hand; it's just not good business. Even at the pathetic savings account rates these days, the interest on a hundred million dollars adds up in one hell of a hurry, and the Feds keep track of every financial transaction exceeding ten thousand dollars. There's only one place I know I can come up with that kind of cash, and if I get caught doing business with him it would be a bigger disaster than everybody finding out how stupid I was with Layla. And the cost! Shit! He's going to bleed me dry!*

*If I don't do it, I risk losing Emily. Jesus! Since her mother passed away Emily is all I have. If anything happened to her it would be the end of everything for me. Hell, if I can't pull this off it's going to be the end of me anyway. The only option I have is one I really don't want to take…*

Turning to the long, low credenza behind his chair, he took out a simple cardboard box in which he kept a half dozen or so burn phones, cheap cell phones he kept for when he had to make the occasional untraceable calls; he lifted one and dialed a number on the Los Angeles exchange.

"¿Hola?"

"¿Sabes quién?" The words, 'You know who" were a password of sorts. The LA number was a relay, and shortly a call would reach out for Ramon Gutierrez in Lima, Peru, to let him know Clarence Harding Larroquette wished to discuss a business deal with him.

*Scott Conrad*

\* \* \*

Emily lay back on the round supersized bed, her naked skin feeling wonderful on the silk sheets. Stretching indolently, she watched out of the corner of her eye as Bykov sat at his dressing table dressed in a short silk smoking jacket, something she recognized only because Daddy had one—only Daddy always wore pants with his. Bykov was smoking a big fat Cuban cigar, just like Daddy did, and he was sipping from a snifter of brandy—Daddy's favorite. She raised her knees and opened them provocatively.

"Kiril?" He glanced over at her and gave her a warm, if brief smile. "I'm still horny." Her knees opened and closed, which she thought was sexy.

*Spoiled,* Bykov thought. *I really expected more of her, given her libidinous proclivities.*

"Perhaps in a bit, my dear. Let me have my brandy and cigar in peace."

"But I'm horny now!" Her legs splayed wide and she reached one slender, elegant hand down between her thighs and caressed her core as she stared up at the mirrored ceiling. Her fingers came away glistening with moisture. She liked being able to watch herself.

*I had not anticipated getting bored with you so quickly, dear, nor expected you to be so tame. You certainly are more inventive when you're with Chloe and Jason. Too bad I only brought Chloe along. It might have been intriguing to watch the three of you together up close.* He pressed a button on his dressing table and a concealed panel in the wall slid open. It was, in fact, an emergency escape route, but in this case it allowed Chloe access to his bedroom when she was summoned.

Barefoot and wearing a sheer teddy designed to enhance her magnificent youthful body, Chloe walked demurely into the room. Her nipples were rigid and poking out against the sheer fabric of the teddy. She came toward him, her movements graceful and feline. When she reached him, she leaned forward as if to embrace him, but he shook his head "no" and nodded toward Emily on the bed. She didn't need any further instruction.

Turning toward Emily, Chloe shrugged one shoulder and allowed one strap of the teddy to fall carelessly down, exposing one tender, small but perfectly formed breast, and then moved swiftly to the massive bed.

"Chloe," Emily purred, extending her arms to embrace the nubile woman.

Chloe, however, had different ideas. She dropped the teddy to the floor and climbed up onto the bed between Emily's outspread knees and started kissing and licking her way down the tanned, shapely thighs.

"Oh!"

Bykov watched the acrobatic display from his dressing table, sipping his brandy and puffing on his cigar. Emily really was getting tiresome. For a wild child, she certainly didn't have a large repertoire. She was far more demanding than she was giving—not at all what a man of refined tastes would prefer. Bykov preferred his women to be a bit more challenging, not so easy to satisfy or even to get into bed. He liked to have to use his skills as a lover to entice, to conquer, and then to excite. In short, Emily Larroquette was simply too easy.

It was time for her to return to her loving Daddy, Bykov had already taken three more hostages in the three weeks Emily had been in his care, but the others had been even more boring than she'd been. Not that they were resistant to his blandishments, quite the opposite. In fact, they were far too easily susceptible.

# Chapter Eight

**Thailand, present day.**

The repatriation of Emily Larroquette and his second and third hostages was more to begin to recoup his massive cash outlays than for his personal pleasure. The hostages had been transported to the monastery in the same manner as Emily had been, though they were drugged at sumptuous dinners and awakened in one of the lavishly renovated monk's cells. Mikhail's use of flunitrazepam, also known as Rohypnol, had been a stroke of genius, though determining the correct dosage was proving a bit tricky. There hadn't been a whisper of publicity and no interest from law enforcement agencies anywhere in the world. The scheme was working better than he'd expected it to.

Flush with his successes, Bykov had targeted two especially lucrative prospects—the trophy wife of a multibillionaire televangelist with a penchant for very young girls that he did not wish to be made public and the daughter of a U.S. senator who'd made hundreds of millions of dollars from lucrative (unethical, and some outright illegal) oil schemes with producers in the Ukraine. If exposed, the illegal transactions alone could get him sent to prison for the rest of his natural life. Both females had reservations within the next two weeks.

\* \* \*

Savannah Aimes, the senator's daughter, was even more beautiful in person than she'd been in her photographs. Bykov watched her carefully from the moment Mai welcomed her. He watched as she undressed for a shower after her long flight from the States, and he had to admit to himself that she was absolutely ravishing without her clothing, a natural beauty in every sense. She was also rather modest, a welcome change from the more uninhibited women who'd come before her. More of a challenge, as Bykov saw it.

He watched approvingly as Savannah dressed in an ordinary yet form-fitting one-piece Lycra swimsuit and donned one of the resort's monogrammed robes before slipping her exceptionally pretty feet into a pair of sleek Italian leather sandals. Her behavior at the pool reinforced his initial impression of her. She sat in Jason's serving area and paid no more than passing attention to the handsome former Mr. Universe. Rather than go for a hard liquor drink, Savannah ordered a bottle of the modestly priced 1998 Veuve Clicquot Ponsardin Champagne Brut La Grande Dame, which showed she was knowledgeable and not just out to impress with expensive tastes.

Bykov was becoming more impressed with her discriminating taste and refinement by the moment. This woman was no pushover; he was intrigued. He would give her a day's breathing space and then invite her to his private sitting room for a small wine and cheese tasting social featuring a choice selection of Malbec wines from Argentine vineyards that paired well with Stilton, Gorgonzola, Camembert, and Brie cheeses. Three more jet-set socialites would be invited as well, but his focus would be on the woman from Austin, Texas, Savannah Aimes. No other guests sparked his interest, but he suspected that Savannah would be dubious if she were the only one invited.

As it turned out, all four women were delighted at the invitation, and all were susceptible to his flattery and his charm. His European manner captivated them, and his impeccable taste in wine impressed the three who were fairly knowledgeable. Savannah spent most of the evening listening rather than talking, but it was she who was most impressed with his knowledge and appreciation for excellent vintages. When it came time for the event to wind down, it was Savannah who lingered.

"That was an impressive display," she said, lifting her wine glass to her lips and taking a tiny sip of a most excellent Malbec. Just the tiniest tip of her pink tongue slipped into the wine before she set the glass down on the crisp white linen cloth covering the wine table. "I'd be curious to see your wine cellar." As simply as that, the trap was sprung. An hour later, she was belted into a passenger seat in the Airbus helicopter, and she, Bykov, and Mikhail were en route to Logovo. When they landed at the monastery, Bykov had special instructions for his right-hand man.

"Take this one to one of the conditioning rooms, Mikhail. We have to handle this one very carefully, she is more discerning than my earlier special guests. Administer a sedative and start the subliminal program as soon as you are certain she is under." Bykov strode away toward his private suite and left Savannah Aimes in the capable hands of Mikhail Orel and two black-suited Chinese orderlies. For the time being, he had plans to enjoy the sole occupant remaining in the renovated monk's cells. She was scheduled to be repatriated in two days anyway and she would be a pleasant diversion during the initial phase of Savannah's indoctrination. The accelerated Stockholm Syndrome training program he had developed and refined had proven remarkably effective.

* * *

The next new candidate came as something of a surprise to Bykov. Pamela Hadley was the spectacularly beautiful (some said "trophy") wife of the Right Reverend Levon Judson Hadley, a renowned televangelist famous for his flamboyant style and extravagant displays of wealth. He traveled with a coterie of bodyguards that looked as tough and mean as they actually were. All were armed at all times.

"The torture scenes have to look real, Mikhail, but I do not wish the women to suffer any real injuries. We must return them blemish-free or we risk retribution—these are powerful men." He had determined that the two men in question were among the most ruthless so far of the relatives of the victims they had selected and that they would require something more convincing than the revelations he planned. The ransom letters had already been delivered, but Bykov had not received a response yet. Both men had platoons of spin-doctors, public relations specialists, that had access to media venues that had enabled them to emerge victorious from scandals before. The senator had survived more than thirty years in Congress, and he was hardened and battle scarred. The preacher, who had a letch for very young girls, had spent enormous sums of cash to successfully keep his peccadilloes out of the press.

Orel acknowledged his instructions with a nod. He was focused on establishing an untraceable net, routed and rerouted through so many different servers and providers that even the NSA (National Security Agency), the United States' most sophisticated communications agency, would be hard pressed to trace a broadcast, provided it was kept short enough. It would be several days before he was satisfied that he had accomplished what he set out to do. Besides, he had done the background investigation into the senator and the preacher, and he doubted very seriously that either could mount an effective attack even on the resort itself, much less Logovo. Nobody knew the connection between the two but Bykov, himself, and the helicopter crew.

* * *

The network was ready. Mikhail had completed the final testing on it that afternoon and declared it untraceable. Bykov was personally seeing to the final preparations on the set where he intended to stage his little drama. The walls of the underground cell, next, incidentally, to his impressive wine cellar, had already greatly resembled those of the interrogation rooms in the Lubyanka, the popular name for the headquarters of the FSB (Federal Security Service of the Russian Federation) and affiliated prison on Lubyanka Square in the Meshchansky district of Moscow. The very name Lubyanka still struck terror into the hearts of Russian citizens, synonymous with its reputation for sadistic torture and murder. That made the cell the ideal setting for Bykov's little drama.

A village blacksmith had been contracted to fabricate a couple of sets of crude black iron shackles, which had then been bolted into the cell walls by the maintenance crew. Instruments of torture from medieval times hung from racks along the walls. A pump-up bottle filled with crimson-dyed water and glycerin sat on the floor between the tripod legs of one of the cameras. Bykov had even sketched a picture of a torture rack from memory and had the maintenance staff construct it of aged lumber from the monastery's storage barn. He'd had them age the device with blow torches and used motor oil until they looked positively ancient. At last, Bykov was satisfied.

Clipping off the end of yet another fat hand-rolled Cuban cigar, he used a gold butane lighter to warm the wrapper before lighting it. He took a couple of puffs, quickly blowing the smoke out of his mouth, until he was satisfied that it was lit and burning properly. Then he ordered everyone out of the room and inspected it a final time from a position behind the camera. Everything was in readiness for the next day. It was time to apply a little more pressure to the senator and the preacher man.

* * *

"Mikhail, is Miss Aimes ready?" Orel had administered a healthy dose of Rohypnol to the socialite an hour earlier.

"I'm sure she is, sir, would you like me to bring her to the dungeon?"

"Yes Mikhail, it's time. Give me a few minutes and I'll meet you there. You know what to do."

Orel bobbed his head in understanding and left Bykov's suite.

Going over to his armoire, Bykov selected a black catsuit identical to the ones used by the FSV. In minutes he was dressed in the catsuit and on his way to the dungeon.

\* \* \*

Savannah moaned. She was wearing nothing but a tee shirt. Her hands were shackled over her head, and the cold black iron surrounding her wrists tore painfully at her skin. Her eyes were glassy and she was unable to focus clearly. Her reactions were sluggish. The dank smell of the wet stone walls was overlaid with something else, a scent that was vaguely familiar. Only when Bykov spoke did she associate the fragrance with the man speaking. Bykov! Sweet woodruff was the primary component of his cologne. Her mind was fuzzy, and she had no control over her body, she couldn't move anything. Her head lolled from side to side weakly, and her eyelids fluttered involuntarily. *What's wrong with me? Why can't I move?*

Another man, not Bykov, one she had never seen before, approached her carrying some kind of plastic sprayer in one hand and a wand in the other. Unable to voice a protest, Savannah's eyes rolled wildly as he sprayed her with some kind of crimson gunk that looked like ... blood. When the man was finished, she heard Bykov speak, though because her brain was functioning so slowly, she couldn't quite understand what he was saying.

The man with the sprayer made an unintelligible response and then set the sprayer down on the floor. He turned, and Savannah's eyes rolled even more wildly as he put his hands inside the neck of her tee shirt and ripped it open down the front so that her breasts were exposed. Horrified, then angry, she began to cry, great tears rolling down her cheeks—exactly the kind of response Bykov was looking for.

Switching the camera on, Bykov picked up a wicked looking riding crop and strode toward the sobbing woman.

\* \* \*

Pamela Hadley received much the same treatment, though her response was far more dramatic. Mikhail Orel donned a black balaclava and contacted both the senator and the televangelist using Skype. He read the ransom demands again tersely and then played the videos in turn. Within 24 hours, Savannah Ames was repatriated, the ransom paid, and there was not a single mention of it in the world press. Levon Hadley was another kettle of fish.

*Track Down Thailand*

\* \* \*

Ko Phai Island is a craggy, wooded island in the Bay of Bangkok. Much of its coast is formed of rocky cliffs, but there are plenty of flat beaches, none of which are regularly patrolled. The entire island is well above sea level, but its highest elevation is only 150 meters, and all of the peaks are about the same. A lighthouse perches on the island's highest peak. Lush vegetation, especially the large bamboo trees, covered the interior that wasn't occupied by Khwām Sukh. The resort had spent lavishly on landscaping, bringing in colorful flowers and trees from the mainland.

The men landed on a white sand crescent-shaped beach on the south end of the island, not far from the tiny village of Hat Thong Lang. The only lights visible were that of the lighthouse and the glow in the sky above Pleasures. The men were all natives of Atlanta, Georgia, home of Reverend Levon Hadley, denizens of the dark side of that fair city. A few of them were veterans of military service, but most were graduates of the School of Hard Knocks, former as well as current members of street gangs. To a man, they were cutthroats and thieves, no strangers to killing and more than willing to do so for money. Knocking over a resort on a tiny island had seemed like a choice plum of a job for the price Reverend Leon had offered, half up front and half on their return. And the guns! Man, the guns! AK-47s, Ingram M-10s ... the big boys that fired .45 cartridges instead of the puny 9mm fired by the M-9. The first reality check hit them just inside the tree line at the edge of the purest white sand beach any of them had ever seen. (It was also the first beach most of them had ever seen.)

"Man, nobody said nothin' 'bout critters! I hate critters." Alfonse Jones had never been in a forest any denser than the trees in Freedom Park in Atlanta.

"Shut up man! We 'sposed ta be observin' noise an' light discipline!" Terrence "T" Banks had been discharged from the U.S. Army after his third AWOL charge in as many months. He'd served for less than a year, but most of the others looked up to him because he was very large and had been 'real Army.' Even the gang-bangers gave him grudging respect—because he knew the lingo and could talk the talk. None of them had ever participated in an organized, military style assault.

After listening to the plan, most of them had felt a little better about their lack of experience—after all, they were just going to roust a few hotel maids and scare a bunch of fancy women with their guns and fierce looks. Business as usual, right? Intimidation usually worked back in the 'hood, and the worst that could happen there was that you had to pop a cap in some dude's ass. As far as any of them knew, there were no gang-bangers in this weird place with all that green shit growing and them damned critters crawling around in the darkness.

"Nobody said *nothin'* about no critters," Jones muttered under his breath. As soon as the words passed his lips, a saw palmetto frond displaced by the man in front of him swung back and smacked him in the face. Saw palmetto has razor-sharp edges, and this one left a tracery of thin cuts on his face. He cursed under his breath as he tasted his own blood.

*This place ain't nothin' like the tropic island paradise that little weasel of a white man promised. I shoulda stayed my ass back in Atlanta! Be jus' my luck he lied about all that fancy pussy jus' there for the takin' at this damn resort place too!* He trudged on, still grumbling inside his head. *That Banks guy, he's known as a mean mother back in the 'hood ... cut you soon as look at you. Bes' keep yo' mouth shut, Jonesie, ya already got paid more green than ya can make hustlin' on the street in three months' time, an' that's just half…*

\* \* \*

Banks led his little band of street thugs through the half klick or so through the lightly wooded area, deliberately picking a path through the densest parts of the forest ahead just to keep the thugs on their toes. *None a them woulda lasted the first week at Fort Benning! Don't matter none, we got this. In an' out, jus' like the Rev said. Jus' gotta bull our way in an' shake down the manager or whoever and fin' out where that sweet thang of a wife a his went to, then we can jet outta here. How hard could that be? Rev said they ain't no men allowed here, so we might jus' take us a lil extra time for some fun an' games with the ladies!* The thought of all those fancy women defenseless in this wilderness caused a stir in his groin, and he adjusted himself as he walked.

His instructions to the men were more for show than anything else. He had been on training patrols during his short stretch in the Army, but he had never led one and he had paid little attention to the instructors at Benning. He did remember hearing one of them say that a night attack by infantry was one of the most difficult tasks a leader could undertake, but that didn't matter on this little island at all. Nothing but yokels and women to worry about here. His little band of thugs looked pretty intimidating. That and the guns should be more than enough to accomplish what he wanted to. Banks smiled to himself. He had doled out a few camouflage sticks and they had painted their faces in garish colors and bizarre patterns, concentrating on the use of the light green at the ends of the camouflage sticks due to the darkness of their own skin. To Banks they looked more like the cast of *The Walking Dead* than they did warriors.

The wooded area gave way to a manicured lawn surrounding the resort complex. Banks could only see one entrance, even though he made a show of taking two men with him on a reconnaissance while the other men lay down in a circle inside the wood line with their weapons pointed outward. He'd admonished them to maintain strict noise and light discipline while he was gone, but upon his return he could see the glow of at least five cigarettes in the darkness and he could hear the laughing and whispering from 200 feet away.

Annoyed at the unprofessional attitude of his crew, Banks barked out an order—a little louder than necessary.

"Quiet!" He glared at them, not that it did any good in the darkness. "it's all clear, and there's only one way in the place. When we come out of the wood line I want everybody spread out, ten feet apart. Weapons locked and loaded and safeties on. Everybody got that?"

A few chuckles greeted his order, and not a few grim smiles. All of them were more than ready to get out of the woods; the heat, the biting insects, and the mysterious rustling noises in the underbrush had them all on edge.

"All right! Everybody out on the lawn and form up in line!"

Their movement out of the wood line was decidedly unmilitary, but Banks was impatient and ready to get started. He stood facing them, fists balled up and resting on his hips, AK-47 slung across his shoulder as he waited for them to form a ragged line to either side of him. Not trusting them, he trooped the line checking to make sure that all safeties were on. Three of them were not and he rudely corrected them. Then he turned, and just like the leader in a John Wayne war movie, he raised his hand above his head and pointed towards the entrance to the resort.

Banks led the way, swaggering in the familiar style of an Atlanta street pimp. They got to within 50 feet of the guard shack before a row of blazing lights suddenly flashed on, bathing them in intense light as well as blinding them. Taken by surprise, Banks and his thugs heard but did not see the concealed garage-size door slide open. The first indication that they were facing armed opposition came with the sound of running feet and the clash of the black clad Chinese impacting their ragged line. Caught completely by surprise, Banks was the first one to go down, and the thugs were leaderless. Jones was the first thug to react, flipping off his safety and touching off the trigger of his M-10 and emptying the magazine on the first pull. His burst was met with but a single aimed shot, which dropped him in his tracks. By then, three more thugs had taken their guns off safe and let rounds fly.

"Huǒ!" (Fire!)

Instantly, accurate, aimed, and withering fire came from the Chinese, and all of Reverend Levon Hadley's street thugs lay dead or dying on the lush green manicured lawn of Pleasures. The lieutenant in charge of the security detail crossed over to where Terrence Banks lay bleeding out and knelt beside him. The last thing "T" saw was the flashing blade of the razor-sharp Ghurka kukri that cleaved his skull cleanly in two.

*"Qīnglǐ zhège lèsè. Wǒ bù xīwàng zài zǎoshang xǐng lái shí kàn dào rènhé jīxiàng!"* (Clean this rubbish up. I want no sign of it visible in the morning when the guests wake up!) The lieutenant, his face a mask of disgust, realized his error too late, and he prodded "T"'s body with the toe of his boot.

*"Kàn kàn shìfǒu yǒu zhèxiē yěmán rén zhī yī hái huózhe. Wǒmen xūyào jiāng qízhōng yīgè sòng huí tāmen de zhǔrén."* (See if there is one of these barbarians still alive. We need to send one of them back to their master.)

\* \* \*

Bykov, he knew, would not be pleased that gunfire had been necessary to subdue the barbarians, but a contingency plan to cover such an eventuality was in place. As the Chinese scurried around to clean up the bloody mess, a single black man with a gunshot wound to the shoulder was spared and the resort physician called out to minister to him. The rest were dumped unceremoniously into the back of two MengShi jeep clones and carried down to the docks, where they were loaded aboard a shrimp trawler and taken out to sea. There, they were fed to the sharks, who seemed to find the flesh of barbarians much to their liking. The trawler captain shuddered as the deed was done. The foreign devil who owned Khwām S̄uk̄h terrified him—he was merciless, not a man to be trifled with.

\* \* \*

Levon Hadley threw a temper tantrum when the sole survivor of his rescue team returned.

"Are you telling me that every one of the men I sent is dead?" he exploded.

The injured survivor, who walked into Hadley's office with a severe limp despite the fact that he had only been wounded in the shoulder, blanched. He flinched as if the good reverend had actually struck him.

"Yeah ... yessir!" Booker Theophilus Washington Jr. began to blubber like a baby. At that moment he wished he had never taken the money from the Reverend Hadley, as a matter of fact he wished he had never heard of Reverend Hadley. "I swear, Rev, they had to be a hunderd of 'em! We almost had 'em! We caught 'em comin' outta that giant garage door in the wall of that resort ... our guys fought like demons, but it wasn't no good. They was Chinese, an' they was all dressed in black like some kinda ninjas! I'm telling ya our guys fought like hell but it was no use. They had what ya call crew served weapons, least ways tha's what Banks called 'em. They mowed us down like we wasn't nothin'!" Washington was cringing, his hands in front of his face as if he were expecting the reverend to strike him. He was gibbering wildly.

"How the hell did you get away?" Hadley roared, his eyes bulging, his face a mottled red, his fists clenched.

Washington lost it.

"I was in the back, man ... they shot me an' I passed out. I ain't lyin'! okay?" He didn't care about the rest of the money he was promised anymore. Hell, he'd be willing to give back what was left of the green the man had already given him—anything to get away from this freeakin' madman. *I shoulda known better than ta trust this white mother! Shoulda listened when my mama tol' me never ta trust a white man...*

Disgusted, Hadley waved the useless thug out of his office. When Washington had left, Hadley looked at his own bodyguard and raised his hand and made a slashing motion across his neck, then nodded his head in the direction of the door that had just slammed shut. The bodyguard, his face impassive, didn't acknowledge the order, he simply turned and went out the door.

His adoring flock would not have recognized the televangelist as he raged around his office, kicking at anything he didn't think would damage his hand-lasted Italian loafers. The last thing he kicked before his fury subsided was a round metal trash can he normally utilized for collecting the contents of his mini paper shredder. Slumping down into his ridiculously expensive ergonomic desk chair, he bent forward, placed his elbows on the green desk blotter, his head in his hands, and concentrated. *That bitch! How could she let herself get kidnapped like that ... or did she? She loves kinky shit like that. Maybe she just did it to get even with me? Nah, she's twisted enough, but she's not that bright. Face it, Levon, you should have known better than to marry a white woman. Can't trust any bitch, especially one that will drop her panties for whoever is willing to spend a lot of money on her. She's been a pain in my ass from the minute that wedding chapel minister in Vegas pronounced us man and wife! Face it, my man, you're going to have to pay through the nose to get her back ... maybe I can negotiate!*

\* \* \*

Bykov sat back in his chair and watched as the two stone-faced Chinese brought the steamer trunk into his office and set it down. He waved his hand in dismissal and the stolid Chinese left wordlessly. He crossed over to the trunk and opened it, staring at the stacks of used hundred-dollar bills. Moving the stacks aside, he found the bottom lined with stacks of one and ten-ounce gold bars, just as Hadley had promised. He smiled to himself. Time enough to return Pamela Hadley to her loving husband after another day or so. She was at that moment lying on her back on his massive four poster bed—in his private suite at Logovo. She was the only female he had ever brought there. Who would have believed that the demure Pamela Hadley would turn into a raging nymphomaniac after being manacled in a dungeon, sprayed with fake blood, and whipped with a stiff leather riding crop? The moment he had taken the manacles off, the woman had fallen to her knees. He'd thought the weeping woman was going to beg for mercy until she'd reached for the zipper on his catsuit. That vixen could do things with her mouth that would give a dead man an erection.

The Aimes woman's repatriation had been a different matter entirely. For some reason she had been resistant to the conditioning program. When she was repatriated, she was furious and had to be taken away in restraints. He'd only taken that one to bed once, in her own cell. She'd been a vicious fighter, nearly scratching his eyes out and leaving bite marks on his shoulder when he'd finally managed to penetrate her and he'd literally forced her into a reluctant but nevertheless massive orgasm. Her convulsions had nearly thrown him, but he'd managed to hold on even though those perfectly capped white teeth had drawn blood. A memorable bout, but not one that he'd care to repeat. Still, she *had* been quite a conquest. What he had no way of knowing was that Savannah Aimes had been a sorority sister of a stunning blonde by the name of Jessica Paul.

# Chapter Nine

**Senator Aimes' Estate, Austin, Texas.**

For several days she refused to come out of her bedroom. Even though the nurse Daddy had hired to look after her was persistent in her efforts to bring Savannah out of her bedroom, Savannah refused to cooperate. She hadn't even permitted the private physician brought out to the senator's residence to examine her. Most of the first day she spent scrubbing herself in the shower, trying to wash the shame off of her skin—but no matter how hard she scrubbed, it wouldn't go away. Without even drying off, she would race to the fairy tale canopy bed and throw herself down on the delicate white silk coverlet, paying no heed to the water stains she was leaving on it. There, she would sob into the silk-covered, down-filled pillows that muffled the sound of her bawling. She cried until her belly hurt and the tears dried up, and then she'd return to the shower, scrubbing her skin raw. The shelves in her bathroom were littered with expensive lotions, ointments, essential oils, and perfumes, but she shunned them—as far as she was concerned, she didn't deserve them.

* * *

"I don't know, senator, I'm at my wits' end." Agatha Sampson, the middle-aged woman who had been hired to care for Savannah, stood in the senator's home office wringing her hands and looking very nervous. She had tried for three days to get Savannah to open her bedroom door to no avail. When the head housekeeper had brought a key the first day to unlock the thick oak door, they had opened it perhaps an inch before a heavy porcelain water pitcher crashed into it and shattered into a million pieces. Savannah had screamed bloody murder, hurling epithets and gutter expletives at the two women until they had made a hasty retreat. Savannah had relocked the door and jammed the lock somehow from the inside. The butler had left food and snacks on a tray outside her door three times a day, but when he returned each time with a new tray, the old one remained where he'd left it, untouched.

The senator, who not only bore but cultivated his resemblance to Colonel Harland Sanders of Kentucky Fried Chicken fame, frowned and leaned back in his desk chair, careful not to spill ash from his cigar on his white Panama suit.

"She's like her mother was, that one. Stubborn as the day is long and ornery as a rattlesnake when you rile her. She certainly didn't get it from my side of the family." Taking the fat cigar between his thumb and forefinger, he carefully set it in the standing ashtray beside his desk. "This is not the first time she has acted out this way, but I'll give you this, she's never been through anything like this before." He put the tips of all his fingers together and regarded the nurse solemnly.

*Track Down Thailand*

"Mrs. Sampson, you can stop worrying now. I could not have asked for better effort from anyone. You've done all you can do, and Savannah is not going to let anybody help her until she is damned good and ready. You go see Mr. Wilkins and tell him I said to pay you for the full week and then you just go on home and rest. Consider the next four days of vacation as a reward for a job well done." Rance Wilkins was the household manager for the senator's large estate. He disbursed all household funds and paid the bills from his office, a small cottage located between the mansion and the horse barn. He also ran the household staff with an iron hand, which was unusual in that he was a small, rather mousy man who might have weighed a hundred and twenty pounds soaking wet.

"That's very generous of you, senator, but you don't have to do that..."

Senator raised his palm. "I know I don't have to do that, Mrs. Sampson, but my daughter has put you through the wringer and you didn't deserve that. Just consider the extra money as hazard pay. Now, you just run along and see Mr. Wilkins with my gratitude." Finished, he returned his attention to the Cuban cigar still burning in the ashtray, the matter of Agatha Sampson already a thing of the past.

*Savannah is spoiled rotten, I have pampered and coddled her from the day she was born. Lord knows I've tried to spend as much time with her as she deserves, but the burden of public service has left me little time to spend with her. The thing is I have got to get a handle on this problem. If those damned reporters get wind of the fact that I paid some son of a bitch a king's ransom to get my daughter back without involving the authorities I am up shit creek. They will smell a story there and they won't stop digging until they find out why, and I simply can't have that in an election year. Oh well, Daddy always said that if you want something done right you have to do it yourself. I'm going to have to take this bull by the horns.*

Senator Aimes groaned, more from mental effort than physical, and rose from his desk chair. Normally he would have taken the staircase up to Savannah's third-floor bedroom, but today he was feeling his age. He walked down the hall to the brass elevator door and punched the up button.

* * *

"Savannah?" He rapped softly on her door.

"Go away!" The tone of her voice was petulant, but the very fact that she had answered him at all told the senator that his daughter was willing to talk. Wishing he had taken a shot of whiskey before coming upstairs, he inserted his master key in the lock and opened her bedroom door.

"Princess?" No response. "Baby, we need to talk."

"I don't want to!" She buried her face even further into her pillow, her voice muffled but clear enough for him to understand.

The senator straightened his shoulders, and the voice that issued from his mouth was the same one he used when addressing his peers on the Senate floor.

"Savannah! Sit up! You're a grown woman and I expect you to act like one."

Recognizing the change in his tone, Savannah slowly raised herself to a sitting position in her bed. When he used that tone of voice, it meant he was deadly serious. "What?" She wasn't quite ready to acquiesce yet. Her tone was still petulant.

"We need to come to an understanding, princess."

"And just what kind of understanding do we need to come to, Daddy?"

"Sweetheart"—his tone mellowed—"nobody can know about what just happened to you. This is an election year, and if my opponents find out that I paid a ransom to that cheap swindler they will drag my good name through the mud until I couldn't win an election for dogcatcher. Baby girl, we stand to lose *everything.* Do you know what that means? *Everything*—the house, the barn, all the horses, that pretty red Porsche of yours ... *everything*!"

"Daddy!" Savannah instantly flew into one hell of a rage. "He *raped* me, Daddy! He beat me with a riding crop and he *raped* me—and you *paid* him?" Her gorgeous face was mottled with rage, her sky-blue eyes clouded and swollen from crying.

"Now just hold on one minute there, princess..." The distinguished gentleman from Texas, Senator Lawrence Bidwell Aimes, had sadly underestimated his daughter's willingness to sacrifice for the sake of her creature comforts or his longtime career in the U.S. Senate. He was reluctantly but seriously contemplating sending her to a private sanitarium outside Austin that he well knew catered to the ultra-rich and famous, keeping the recalcitrant spouses and children out of the public eye to avoid scandals for their significant others. Politics was a dirty game, but it was his—and he could not afford any chinks in his armor. He had plenty of enemies who would have a field day with the information that rapist of a kidnapper had.

*I don't want to do that to my baby girl, I hate the thought of it; on the other hand, I've no intention of losing this office or, worse, spending the rest of my life in Federal prison ... much less losing everything I've worked for over the last forty years. St. Elizabeth's is damned expensive, but I know very well that she'd be given the best of care there—and she wouldn't be permitted any communication with the outside world.*

He was just about to mention the name of the place, a veiled threat, when Savannah's rage suddenly subsided.

"I'm sorry, Daddy, it's just ... you don't understand how humiliating that was for me." She was still sniffling. "And he hurt me, Daddy!" She was still seething inside, but she had seen the expression on his face and she *knew* what he was thinking. St. Elizabeth's. The place where Senator Bramble's wife had been taken after her drinking and wild parties threatened to screw up his chances at re-election. They called it a rehabilitation sanitarium, but in actuality it was a prison for family members who were rocking the boat. Her friend, Mary Sommers, had spent almost a year in the ultra-luxurious sanitarium and had regaled her with the details ... forced curfew, no communication with *anybody* outside the grounds, nothing. Savannah had no intention of spending a single moment at St. Elizabeth's ... but she wasn't about to forget what that Russian bastard had done to her. Imprisoning her and beating her with that riding crop had been horrible enough, but what had humiliated her most was that he'd made her climax ... the most incredible sex she'd ever experienced. She'd hated herself for what she was doing, but she had abased herself even further by begging him to come back and do it again. Her humiliation was complete when he refused to come back to her monk's cell for more.

*Oh yes, he's going to pay dearly for that ... and so will you, Daddy dear!* Her eyes downcast to conceal the fury in them, Savannah turned her head slightly away from her father's pointed gaze.

"I understand, Daddy, I won't tell."

"Just to make sure we are clear, princess, you can't tell anybody, not a living soul. Do you understand? We could lose *everything*!"

"I *said* I understand, Daddy, you don't have to yell at me!" Her anger was threatening her self-control, so she stood up and crossed over to the senator and hugged him. Turning her head to one side, she laid it against his chest and felt his arms tightening around her. Once upon a time, the gesture would've been reassuring. If the senator could have seen the look on her face he would have had her committed to St. Elizabeth's on the spot.

* * *

After the senator left her room, she refused to think of him as "Daddy" anymore. She called downstairs and ordered a huge meal of steak with mushrooms, French fries, and a fresh garden salad. The meal was delivered in record time and she ate ravenously. A tall glass of iced tea was delivered with food, and she drank half of it before going to her lingerie drawer and withdrawing a bottle of liquor. The bottle had been concealed there since her junior year in high school. If the upstairs maid had ever said anything about it to the senator, he had never mentioned it. Savannah poured a heavy dollop of the bourbon into the tea and stirred it with her finger. She took a sip and then poured another dollop of bourbon into the glass.

*Unbelievable! His own daughter is kidnapped and raped and he says, 'Don't tell anybody'! What kind of father would do that? I have to be careful, I know that. I've got to figure out how to do this without him getting suspicious. That Russian son of a bitch has to pay! I have to find someone to help me, someone who will not be afraid of the senator, someone who can make sure Bykov will be punished.*

*I'm not just thinking of myself. What about all those other women in cells? I wish I could remember their names; hell, I wish I had bothered to find out their names. That one they brought in to be tortured beside me, I know I've seen her face before, I just can't remember where! She was pretty, I'll give her that.*

Her pretty features screwed up into a fierce scowl. Bykov had gone back to that slut all right. She listened to the sounds of passion coming from the cell adjacent to hers. All night long, Bykov had pleasured the gorgeous blonde woman, making her cry out in ecstasy—while Savannah lay in her twin bed, alone in her cell, wishing it had been her Bykov was thrusting into so enthusiastically. Crying with shame, she had touched herself frantically until she reached the most frustrating orgasm of her life. It had been all she could do to refrain from crying out at the end.

*What was her name? I know I've seen that face before, on TV I think … God, I wish I could remember!*

It would be two days before she saw that face again. It was on the nightly news. Savannah looked up from her college yearbook and saw the blonde standing next to that black televangelist, Levon something … Hadley. The Reverend Levon Hadley! Savannah booted up her laptop and, sitting cross-legged on her bed, googled the good reverend. The blonde's name was Pamela, and she was the wife of one of the most powerful televangelists in the country! Interesting. There was no mention of a kidnapping or ransom. Not a single word.

\* \* \*

She was looking up her sorority sisters in her senior yearbook. The best and closest true friends she'd ever had were the ones she had made in her sorority house at the University of Texas. The list of names on her sorority's page read like a Who's Who of the best and brightest Texas had to offer. Millionaire socialites, daughters of men influential in politics, the oil industry, in banking and finance, all were well represented—but which one would be most likely to help her in this situation? She needed somebody fearless, somebody who was not afraid to buck the status quo. Somebody who would not back down because of powerful opposition, but who?

Halfway down the page she found her answer. Fearless, a champion of the oppressed. If she remembered correctly, this young woman had bucked the system frequently through all four years of college. She'd always been in the thick of things, either for or against something or other. She had run for student body president her senior year and had lost out to a popular idiot, one who had won the title of Miss Texas in a beauty pageant. Savannah also remembered that the young woman had been an adventuress, a treasure hunter.

*Jessica Paul! I wonder whatever became of her. I seem to recall her being involved in breaking up some child exploitation scheme down in South America somewhere. Peru maybe?*

After several hours of searching the web, she found the story she was looking for. It was an obscure government report from the Department of State. It was an annotation to the report on travel conditions in the Amazon basin. A child abduction ring that specialized in selling young girls into sexual slavery had been broken up by some character from Dallas, a retired Marine. Jessica Paul had been involved, but the report did not specify exactly how.

Interesting. Now all she had to do was find a phone number for Jessica Paul.

# Chapter Ten

**Jacobs Ranchette, present day.**

The coals from the mesquite fire were the exact color needed to roast the beef quarter turning on the spit above it. Ving stood beside the beef, basting it with a marinade made from a recipe that he absolutely refused to identify.

"I can't tell you, Vicky. It's an ol' family secret, I got it from my granddaddy, an' I swore I would only pass it on to my oldest son. I can tell you for sure, though, you ain't never tasted beef this sweet and tender in your natural life." He dipped the long-handled brush into the small black iron kettle beside the fire, coating the head with the oily reddish liquid and then raising it to baste the slowly turning meat.

"Come on, Ving, you can tell me. I'm not going to give away your secret! My God that smells heavenly!"

Ving lifted his icy cold glass of Wild Ale from Jester King Brewery to his lips with his free hand, continuing to baste the meat with the fragrant sauce.

"Nope," he said after a healthy swallow. "I swore a blood oath to that ol' man. I swear I believe he would rise up outta his grave an' haunt me for the rest of my life if I broke that oath!"

"Ving, you don't really believe that."

Ving eyed the tall, slender, green-eyed redhead standing next to him holding her own glass of beer. "My granddaddy was a gen-u-wine N'awlins Obeah man, an' yes I believe that. If you'd a growed up in N'awlins you'd believe it too. Things in that city ain't the same as they are other places. Strange things happen down there that folks from *away*, rational folks, jus' can't comprehend." He took another swallow, a faraway look in his eyes. "I seen things with these eyes you wouldn't hardly believe." As he always did when he was telling tales about his hometown, he had slipped into the speech patterns and vernacular of his childhood.

"Give up, Vicky." Brad laughed. "When he gets like that, there's no reasoning with him."

"Don't make fun of him, Brad," admonished Willona. "He really believes some of that nonsense. I can never be sure whether he's telling the truth or spinning a yarn when he gets like this."

"Obeah man ain't no joke," Ving said seriously. "People who vexed Obeah man paid for it, an' nobody crossed him an' got away with it!" He shuddered as if remembering something horrible.

Brad walked up behind Vicky and wrapped his arms around her waist, pulling her close and nuzzling her neck playfully.

"Humor him," he whispered softly into her ear. "Ving really does believe some of that mumbo-jumbo from his childhood, and he gets upset when you call him on it." Ving upset was something nobody liked to see. The big man was rarely cross … usually a jovial fellow, easy to get along with. When he was upset, he was never mean to his friends, but he was a master at pouting.

"Yeah, you don't wanna get him started on that Voodoo stuff, Vicky." Jared spoke from a lawn chair safely out of Ving's reach, Fly sitting on his lap and sipping from a beer of her own.

"Stop picking at the man, Jared," Pete Sabrowski piped up. "I don't find his belief in the supernatural to be so different than your superstitious shooting rituals." Jared refused to take a long shot with a sniper rifle without first wetting his thumb and rubbing it across his front rifle sight, even when he was using a powerful scope and not the sight post. He also carried his Marine Corps marksmanship badge on a leather thong around his neck, touching it for luck before shooting, even in a desperate firefight.

Jessica, sitting with Charlie on a bench near the fire, watched the humorous interplay among the close-knit group with quiet amusement. Each and every one of them had their personal quirks, peculiarities they observed before going into action. She had seen them so many times that she would have been disturbed if they'd failed to perform them. Her cell phone rang just as she was about to say that, and she held up a finger to Charlie to indicate that she was moving away from the noise to take the call. She walked into the darkness some distance away from the fire while the discussion continued, interspersed with quiet laughter as one or another of them made witty remarks.

"Hello?"

"Is this Jessica Paul?" It was a cultured voice that Jess found vaguely familiar.

"Yes it is, who's calling?"

"It's me, Jess, Savannah Aimes."

"Savannah! Hi! I thought I recognized that voice. It's been so long! How in the world are you?" There was a pregnant pause before Savannah answered.

"I could get in real trouble with my daddy for talking to you about this, Jess, but I'm so mad I don't care anymore!"

"Whoa! Calm down, Savannah! What's going on?" Jessica remembered Savannah Aimes as a very quiet, peaceful girl who rarely got upset about anything ... an easygoing person with a cheerful personality and a kindly manner. She'd actually been one of those sorority girls that had been so saccharin sweet that Jessica'd had little to do with her, preferring the company of her more active sorority sisters.

"Have you ever heard of a resort in Thailand called *Khwām Sūkh*? It translates as Pleasures."

"Sure, my friend Vicky and I have been talking about going for a stay there."

"Don't go there!" Savannah sounded distraught. "Listen Jess, I heard you were somehow involved in breaking a child slavery ring down in Peru."

Jessica rarely discussed Team Dallas with what she considered "civilians"; it was beyond the capacity of most of her friends to comprehend what Jessica did for a living. That was one of the primary reasons why Jess didn't stay in close contact with any of her friends from college. They'd had a difficult enough time understanding her treasure hunting career. None of them would have understood the lure of combat, the tremendous feeling of satisfaction she got from working with Team Dallas, that she felt at rescuing hostages from the clutches of evil men.

"Yes," Jessica admitted cautiously. "I was involved in that, but my part in it was no big deal..." *Not unless you count me dispatching that bastard Gutierrez anyway!*

"Listen Jess, I heard there was some kind of outfit here in Texas that handles ... sensitive situations like that, kidnappers, you know?"

"Yes," Jessica said hesitantly. "I might have an idea who they might be." Team Dallas did not advertise. The people who required their services found out about them by word of mouth, mostly from satisfied clients.

"This is important, Jess, really it is. I went to Pleasures because I had several friends rave about the place."

"Okay..."

"I was kidnapped, Jess, held for ransom by a sadistic Russian jerk named Bykov!"

"What?"

"Daddy paid the ransom, Jess, but he's forbidden me to tell anybody about it because it's an election year and he's afraid if it gets out that he paid off that scumbag it might cost him the *election!*" There was a sob over the connection and then Savannah blurted out. "Jess, he raped me and then he made my daddy pay a fortune to get me back!" A louder sob. "I'm not the only one either! There are more women still there!"

"Wait a minute, Savannah, slow down. Start at the beginning and tell me everything..."

\* \* \*

"Vicky? Have you got a minute?"

Vicky turned away from the group conversation to see Jessica beckoning to her from the shadows. Curious, she went to see what Jessica wanted.

"What's up, Jess?" The night air was cool but not cold, and the Texas sky was clear and filled with stars that one could never see in Dallas. Both women were dressed casually in jeans and sweaters.

"I just got the weirdest call from one of my sorority sisters from college."

"Prank? Fundraiser?"

"Nothing like that, Vicky. She told me she'd been kidnapped!"

"Now? Do you know where she is?" Vicky's shrewd mind was instantly filled with a million questions.

"No, she's been released. Her father paid the ransom."

"I guess it's too late for us to do anything about it now. Where did it happen? Has she called the FBI?"

"One question at a time, Vicky, let me explain. She was at the resort we were talking about, Pleasures. It's run by some Russian guy, Bykov I think she said."

"Kirill Bykov?" Vicky's eyes widened and she leaned forward eagerly. Kirill Bykov was a name she knew well. A former *Polkovnik* in the FSV, he had left the Russian spy service under curious circumstances and had later turned up as a Russian Mafia don. Vicky's contacts in the CIA were of the opinion that Bykov was holding something over the head of his superiors high up in the FSV. In any case, his defection from the Russian Mafia had been even more suspicious. Word was that he had amassed a huge fortune and struck out on his own, but no one in the intelligence community had the remotest idea where he might have landed. Vicky's interest in him stemmed from her study of Russian experiments in instilling and accelerating the effects of Stockholm Syndrome in hostages.

"I don't know, she didn't say. All she told me was that it was a Russian guy named Bykov. Anyway," Jessica continued, "my friend says he has several hostages still in his clutches."

"Did she say where? Is he holding them at the resort?"

"No, she said she was blindfolded and taken somewhere in a helicopter but she has no idea where. She said when they turned her over to her dad they were on a yacht somewhere in the Bay of Thailand."

Vicky moved her head closer to Jessica's. "Are you sure this isn't some kind of wild-ass gag, Jess? Do you believe her?"

Jessica dropped her eyes from Vicky's steady gaze.

"I don't know. She was a goody two-shoes back in college. She didn't drink to excess or do drugs that I knew of. Her daddy is a powerful man and rich to boot. I know she was pampered and spoiled."

"Yes, but do you believe her?"

"I'm pretty sure I do. She dropped a name, one that I recognized right off. Pamela Hadley, you know, the wife of that televangelist who's always begging for money to feed and clothe the poor while wearing a ten-thousand-dollar Armani suit."

"What about her?"

"My friend says Mrs. Hadley was held and tortured at the same time she was, only Mrs. Hadley developed a serious crush on the Russian in a very short time despite being held hostage. I remember seeing her on television last night with her husband. She did not look very happy to be there."

Vicky pondered what Jessica had told her for a moment then turned to Brad and beckoned for him to come over to her.

"Brad, Jessica has just told me something very disturbing and I want her to repeat it to you. Keep in mind that Kirill Bykov is former SFV *and* a former Russian Mafia don." She turned her head to Jessica. "Tell him what you told me."

Brad listened to his cousin as she explained the whole situation to him as best she could.

"Who is this girl, Jess?"

"Brad, she told me this in confidence. She said she'd get in a lot of trouble if her daddy finds out she's said a word about it to anybody."

Brad glanced back at Vicky and then his cousin one more time and then shook his head.

"I don't know, Vicky. It's a good yarn, but there's not enough there to justify Team Dallas mounting an operation." He turned his attention to his cousin. "We don't normally take on investigations without being asked to by the victims or their relatives."

"You took on Ainsley up in Wyoming," Jessica retorted.

Brad shook his head. "That was different. We *saw* Ainsley being chased, and we recognized both him and his pursuer. We had no choice, it was going down right in front of us." He thought for a moment. "I'll tell you what. You get with Fly and get me some hard intel. Then give me some names. You already got Pamela Hadley, you can start with her." Then he turned and went back to the Mesquite fire, grabbing another craft beer on the way.

Vicky and Jessica did a little research of their own late into the night. What they discovered piqued Vicky's curiosity even further. Early the next morning, they approached Fly in her new lab.

\* \* \*

"Bykov? Is one sure we are talking about Kirill Bykov?"

"Not a hundred percent sure, but the profile and the description fit to a T."

"I knew that bastard would turn up somewhere," Fly fumed. "If you'd heard half the stories I've heard about him it would make you sick." She balled up her fist and slammed it down on top of her brand-new desk.

"Brad says we have to get him names. Jess, you've given us one already with serious name recognition—Pamela Hadley. We'll start with her, but if she doesn't give us any other names we can use you're going to have to give up your friend's name."

"I don't know, Vicky…"

"It's the only way, Jess. Otherwise, you're just pissing into the wind." The pithy masculine remark came from Fly, the daintiest, most demure looking one of the trio. In Fly's case, looks could be deceiving.

# Chapter Eleven

**Logovo, present day.**

Mikhail Orel was perspiring heavily. With Bykov's recent acquisitions, his workload had increased dramatically. He was not only faced with his background investigations and computer duties, he was also responsible for the care and feeding of seven spoiled and pampered beauties—to include supervising their indoctrination into Bykov's accelerated Stockholm Syndrome conditioning. He was putting in twenty-hour days, something he had not had to do since his days with the FSV as Bykov's deputy. Nearing the end of his rope, he approached Bykov and admitted he was beginning to fall behind.

"Mikhail, comrade, you should have spoken sooner!" Bykov smiled expansively and clapped Orel on the back with one broad manicured hand.

"Call the resort and tell Serzhant Moroz he is being reassigned to Logovo. Serzhant Chorney can handle supervising the cultural aides at the resort by himself, he speaks Mandarin fluently. Have him come back here tomorrow morning on the helicopter. He can take over your babysitting chores, but I will still need you to supervise the conditioning program. That should free up some of your time."

"Thank you, sir, that will be a tremendous help." It was not as much relief as Mikhail had hoped for, he was still faced with the helicopter trip to and from Logovo seven days a week. He was a little disappointed, but he allowed none of it to show on his face. Dismissed, he turned to leave.

"Mikhail?" Orel turned again to face his employer. Bykov smiled once more, even wider this time. "Bring your own things back on the chopper in the morning. You can do your background investigations from the comm center here. I want you to take one of the guest suites and remain here at Logovo until further notice. Morov can take one of the cells." Orel nodded and started to leave again. He made it almost to the door before Bykov stopped him once more. "Mikhail, my old friend, bring back one of the masseuses to tend to your, ah, personal needs." The two men smiled knowingly at each other. Mikhail was satisfied.

Bykov studied the retreating back of his number two. It was time for Moroz to assume more of Mikhail's duties anyway. The senior sergeant had served over long as an enlisted man, he had earned the right to assume the duties of a junior officer by dint of his long service. Satisfied that he had solved a minor problem both wisely and decisively, Bykov contemplated his latest successes somewhat smugly.

The addition of several new hostages over a period of weeks had resulted in two more hostile incursions by paid security personnel, both considerably more professional than the ones sent by that fool Hadley. His 'cultural aides' at the resort had handled the new incursions with far less bloodletting than the first one. Most of the invaders had been chained and spirited off to China, where they had been sold into slavery. Two had been sent back to their masters with well-staged videotapes of hostages and sufficient injuries to ensure that there would be no repeat incursions. Bykov was pleased.

He was also pleased with his choice of the Airbus H-225 helicopter. The extended range of the specially equipped chopper, along with its abundant power, enabled it to fly at wave top level, beneath radar detection. Because of the excellence of the bird and the superior skills of his carefully selected pilots, no one had discovered the location of Logovo. Thus far, his scheme was succeeding far beyond his expectations. The conditioning program was working perfectly. Since the Aimes woman, every one of the captives had succumbed to the conditioning program to one extent or another. Savannah had given him a moment or two of real passion, but he had known she was sharper than his average guest. It was for that reason that he had refused her when she had begged him to return to her cell. The woman was dangerous and he had needed to get rid of her as soon as possible.

The others had provided him with a steady stream of conquests, some more delightful than others, but all pleasant enough. He was hard-pressed to keep them all satisfied despite his virility and his incredible stamina in the boudoir, but he had been forced to bring Jason over from *Pleasures* and include him in the conditioning program. That ploy had been a master stroke of genius. It had also enabled Bykov to be more discriminating in his choice of bedmates. All the pieces of the plan were fitting together and working like a well-oiled machine. It was time to retire to his private suite for his brandy and cigar, after which he would make his decision about which captive he would enjoy that evening.

* * *

Vassily Moroz whistled happily as he packed his bags to go to Logovo. He knew it was unprofessional of him, but he hated the Chinese 'cultural aides' with a passion born of three years' service on the Sino-Soviet border before the fall of the Soviet Union. Most people in the world were blissfully unaware that a real live shooting war had been going on along that boundary for nearly seventy years. He was aware, of course, that there were substantially more 'cultural aides' at Logovo, but he had been informed by Kapitan Orel that he would no longer be required to have contact with them at all. They were garrisoned in a separate part of the monastery and spent the majority of their time outside honing their military skills. Moroz would be quartered with the serving staff. His distaste for the Chinese did not extend to the diminutive Thai women on the staff, and he had enjoyed dalliances with several of them at *Pleasures.*

* * *

"Getting to Pamela Hadley is turning out to be much harder than I expected." Fly sighed. Vicky, Jessica, and Fly were sitting at a marble-topped counter in the Weekend Coffee Shop at the Joule on Commerce Street in Dallas sipping cappuccinos and nibbling at an assortment of delicious, if small, pastries.

"That husband of hers has a slick IT department, I'll tell you that for sure. I had a hell of a time cracking his RSA (Rivest–Shamir–Adleman) 4096 bit encryption system. His encryption key is public and it's different from the decryption key, which is not. On top of that, once I got inside, I found that every file folder has a code name that does not specify what's inside it ... and there are literally millions of files in that sucker. He spent some big—

and by big I mean enormous—bucks for that computer of his. Somehow he got hold of an older Cray supercomputer, and he's running me ragged. Right now I'm having to break into millions of files and search each one until I find what I'm looking for. I don't know how they do it!" She shook her head in aggravation. Every bit of her own considerable computer power was methodically breaking down Hadley's individual files and using a search algorithm she had developed on her own at NSA to ferret out specific information she was looking for. So far she had come up with nothing because many of the files were filled with random gibberish. Some IT geek had spent a great deal of time and effort to set the system up. It was enough to make her hair turn gray.

"What are we going to do?" Jessica asked pointedly.

"Find another way to get Mrs. Hadley's private itinerary for starters," Fly retorted. "I'll find it, but at this rate it won't be 'til next Christmas!"

"There has to be a way to figure out where Pamela Hadley is going when she's not with her wacko husband." Vicky was racking her brain for options.

A waitress setting napkins in a holder beside them at the counter laughed delightedly.

"Why shucks, sugar! That ain't no big secret. Everybody knows Pamela Hadley—her maiden name was Burris you know—grew up in West Dallas. Her mama still lives there too. Poor thing! You'd think as much money as Pam spends on clothes and beauty parlors—Raylene told me she heard it was in the *hundreds* of thousands of dollars—she'd be able to buy her mama a decent place to live instead of that ramshackle old house she lives in now! I swear! Ain't it a shame how some people get rich and forget all their old friends and their poor old parents?"

"Excuse me—" Vicky looked pointedly at the waitress's name tag "—Dottie. Are you telling me you know where Pamela Hadley's mother lives?"

Dottie laughed. "Land sakes! 'Course I do. I grew up down the street from Pam Burris. We went to school together our whole lives!"

"So do you think her mother would be willing to tell us how we could get hold of Pamela when she's away from her husband?"

Dottie stared at the three of them as if she thought they were crazy. "You don't have to ask her mama that. Pam may have put on a lot of airs since she married that rich, colored preacher, but she don't neglect to visit her mama and carry that poor woman down to Mama June's Beauty Parlor every Saturday morning!"

# Chapter Twelve

**Texas, present day.**

No one would have recognized the famous Pamela Hadley as she walked through the door of the nondescript greasy spoon restaurant on Dallas's west side. Her glorious mane of blonde hair was pulled back into a tight bun and covered with a cloche hat. Her piercing blue eyes were hidden by enormous sunglasses, and her svelte body was covered with a modest print dress that would not have been out of place in one of the local grocery stores. She had borrowed the car of one of her housemates before leaving home, a 10-acre estate in North Dallas.

Not taking off her sunglasses, Pamela took a quick glance around the seating area and spotted a slender green-eyed redhead who looked like a high fashion model and a younger athletic blonde who was just as pretty sitting together at a table for four. Wasting no time, she walked over to the table where the pair was sitting and addressed the redhead.

"Excuse me, are you Vicky?"

Vicky Chance flashed her engaging smile and nodded. She had agreed over the phone not to use Pamela's name at any time as a condition for the interview. Sighing with relief, Pamela sat down across from the two women and set her large handbag on the vacant chair beside her.

"How did you know?" she whispered. Just as Vicky was about to respond, a tired-looking waitress approached the table with her order pad and pen.

"Would y'all like to order now?"

"Iced tea for all of us," Vicky ordered. When the waitress left, disappointed that they hadn't ordered food, she turned back to Pamela. "I hope that's all right with you."

"Perfectly." Pamela had absolutely no intention of letting anything from this establishment pass her lips anyway. "Who told you? How did they know?"

The blonde woman responded to her question with a question of her own. "Does it really matter? We know; that's why you came here today."

"If this gets out my reputation will be ruined, and, besides, my husband would divorce me and I'd have to go back to living in this rathole!" She waved in the general direction of outside.

Vicky dropped her voice so low that even Jessica could barely hear her. "Listen, there are other women in danger right now, don't you think that's worth more than your reputation? Besides, your husband can't blame you for something done to you against your will."

Pamela Hadley lowered the sunglasses on her nose and stared directly into Vicky's eyes. "Honey, when you told me that you knew what happened at

Pleasures, I took you at your word. I panicked, and I went to a lot of trouble to get here, apparently for no reason. I'm going home." She started to get up.

Vicky's arm shot out and grasped her by the wrist. "You're just going to walk away and leave those other women in mortal danger?"

"Are you crazy? The only danger those women are in is of getting the most mind-bending sex they've ever had!" The look on Pamela Hadley's face was one of pure disdain. "Now, if you don't mind letting go of my wrist, I need to get back to the estate before that lunkhead husband of mine gets suspicious."

"Wait a minute," Jessica cried, confusion on her face. "Why did you come here if you didn't want to have those bastards caught and punished?"

The look on Pamela's face turned to disgust. "Punished? Honey, that is the sexiest man I've ever seen, and he's hung like a bull! Punished? Hell, I'd pin a medal on him if I could, and if I can figure out a way to get back in that bed of his I will do it. As for why I came here, I signed a stupid-ass prenuptial agreement before Levon Hadley would marry me. If he finds out I willingly spread my legs for Kirill—not once but every night for days, all night long—I'd be out on the streets on my ass with nothing but the clothes on my back!" Angry now, she stood and walked out the door, leaving Vicky and Jessica staring after her open-mouthed.

\* \* \*

Despite the Texas heat, Vicky drove the new shadow-black Shelby GT 500 Mustang with both windows rolled down and the air conditioner going full blast. They were halfway back to the ranchette before Jessica blurted out in anger, "What a total waste of time! I can't *believe* Savan ... my friend lied to me! Why would she do that?"

"Don't be in such a hurry to doubt your friend, Jess. Pamela Hadley wouldn't be the first woman to fall for her captor. You've heard of Stockholm Syndrome?"

Jessica stared at her friend. "I've heard of it, but I've never been sure it wasn't BS."

"Oh, it's not BS, believe me, and Kirill Bykov was working on a method for accelerating that psychological effect to the point where he could control someone within a matter of days before he left the FSV. Word in the Intelligence community was that he stole his own program when he cut loose from the Russian security agency."

"That doesn't make sense, Vicky. Wouldn't they have just killed him and kept his program to themselves? Developing that program had to have cost a fortune."

Vicky shrugged as she slowed the Mustang and took the turnoff to the ranchette. "Not if he had something on his superiors, and Fly is pretty sure he did. You're right, the FSV is not the most forgiving agency in the world."

"Does that crap really work? I mean it's hard to believe a woman like Pamela Hadley would fall for it."

"Oh, it works all right. Stockholm Syndrome is very real, and given enough time it occurs without any effort by the principal at all. If half of what I've read about Kirill Bykov is true, I don't have any trouble believing he could bend a woman like Pamela to his will and make her fall in love with him. His work in studying the root causes of the syndrome is ground-breaking, at least the work he's published is. And have you seen a picture of him?"

"No, I just read Fly's synopsis of his dossier."

"He's god-awful gorgeous, very suave, with European manners and dresses like a male high fashion model. Even without the psychological conditioning women seem to throw themselves at him. According to everything I've heard, he's quite the ladies' man."

Jessica smiled wickedly. "She said he was hung like a bull…"

"So I heard," Vicky said drily as she tooled the Mustang into the driveway leading behind the barn. There was no sign of the men of Team Dallas outside as she brought the black car to a full stop and rolled the windows up.

"I guess I need to read that dossier myself," Jessica muttered, opening the car door. "Let me go check with Fly."

"I'll be in in minute."

Jessica didn't answer, she was already opening the new steel office door the contractor had installed to give Fly easier access to her new lab.

Vicky climbed out of the car and leaned back against the fender, her mind racing. She watched a cardinal hopping along the white board corral beside the barn. It stopped and bent to the grass, pecking at some insect on the ground, then raised and cocked its head, staring at her quizzically. After a moment, it lost interest in her and hopped on in search of more food.

*There is definitely something going on at Khwām Sūkh! I wasn't convinced when Jess told me her friend's tale, but when I heard Bykov's name, I got suspicious. That was a shocker all right. Never expected to hear from that bastard again, not after he crossed both the FSV and the Russian mob! I figured he was probably dancing with the fishes at the bottom of the Caspian Sea by now. The Hadley woman confirmed my hunch that it was the same Bykov when she called him Kirill.*

*That still won't be enough to satisfy Brad's need for intel, but it's sure as hell enough for me to dig deeper. With Bykov involved there's no doubt in my mind that something stinks to high heaven. I'm not really sure how to go about this, but maybe Fly will be able to point me in the right direction. She was even closer to the spook community than I was, and she was in it a lot longer than I was...*

\* \* \*

"Yes, Pamela Hadley confirmed that Kirill Bykov was the guy who had her, but get this, he *had* her in the biblical sense, and she definitely wants more! She's not in the least interested in punishing the man, she's more worried about her husband finding out what she was doing while she was at Pleasures." Jessica shook her head in disbelief. "Can you *believe* that?"

"After living in D.C. so many years I would believe anything. Women like that are a dime a dozen there." Fly was digging in a stack of manila folders. She grunted when she found the one she wanted and then handed it to Jessica. "Here, read this." Jessica took the proffered folder and began to read the details of Kirill Bykov's life.

Vicky crossed over the lab and looked over Jessica's shoulder.

"Bykov?"

"Yeah. Fly just gave this to me."

"Read it, especially the part about his service with FSV's Psy-Ops Division. He's a smart bastard."

Jessica let out a low whistle as she uncovered a photograph of the man. He bore a remarkable resemblance to Jonathan Goldsmith, the actor who played the original "most interesting man in the world" in commercials for *Dos Equis* beer.

"Yeah, a lot of women have that reaction to the slick bastard. That's one of the things that makes him so effective—and so dangerous." She shuddered.

"I met him once," Fly said quietly. "It was at a party in D.C., some senator was trying to line his pockets on a wheat deal. I already knew enough about the man to be repulsed by him, but that didn't stop me from having an embarrassing physical reaction to the bastard. His eyes are ... hypnotic. He has a charisma that is difficult—to say the least—to resist. Women are drawn to him like moths to a candle flame."

"We don't have any idea how many women he's victimized, Fly. I need to figure out a way to identify them and get in touch with them."

Fly bent over her computer keyboard for several minutes, focused with an intensity that excluded everything and everyone around her.

"Well, she's gone for the time being."

Vicky chuckled. "Don't disturb her, Jess, she's on a roll. I'll bet that when she comes back to the land of the living she'll have come up with a way I can identify and contact those women."

"We," Jessica retorted. "We! No way you're going to do this alone, Vicky. It was me who started this and I'm in."

Vicky fixed her sea-green eyes on Jessica's blue ones. "If you're in, then give ... what's your friend's name? I'm going to have to know anyway if we're going to interview her."

"I don't know…"

"You said you're in. It's all or nothing, Jess. Either give up her name or I'll go it alone."

Chastened, Jessica reluctantly complied.

"Wow! The chairman of the Armed Services Committee?"

Jessica nodded.

"Aimes?" Fly's head jerked up and she stared at the two women. "What's that dirty old bastard up to now?"

"It was his daughter that told Jess about the kidnappings."

"He's definitely a sleazeball. Bykov must have had some really good dirt on him for that feisty old rooster to pay a ransom, even for that spoiled rotten daughter of his. Wonder what it was."

"We can figure that out later, Fly; for now we need to figure out how to contact those women," Vicky said evenly.

"Hold your horses, Vicky, I'm already working on that. I'm hacking into the Khwām Sukh mainframe as we speak. I had a little trouble locating it, it's not at the Ko Phai Island location. When I hit the mainframe there, I found a feed from another mainframe that I can't pin down, it's basically ... nowhere."

"How can that be?"

"Floating IP address. Tricky as hell, but all I have to do is penetrate it while it's active at one address and I'm in. I still won't be able to pinpoint a physical location, but I will be able to piggyback the computer wherever it's at once I'm inside." She had developed that little software gem on her own, and she had nicknamed it "The Leech" because that was what it did. Normally she could access a program from NSA that would give her a physical location, but whoever had designed the Khwām Sūkh network was a bona fide programming prodigy. So far the NSA software had been stymied. "It doesn't really matter at the moment, I can get the guest list from the Ko Phai mainframe."

"That's great, Fly, but don't give up on trying to track down the physical location. I'll bet anything you want to that the physical location of that other mainframe is where they are holding the hostages. Brad's going to want to know that."

In less than an hour Fly produced a hard copy of the guest list covering the time from the day Pleasures had opened its doors.

This time it was Fly who let out a low whistle. "Who would ever have guessed there were so many multibillionaires on this planet?"

"They're not all multibillionaires," Jessica pointed out. "I recognize some of these names. A lot of them are just filthy rich, even if they are all jet-setters."

"Narrow it down for us, please. I need … we need to weed out all but the wealthiest of these guests, say the top twenty percent. Can you do that, Fly?"

"Give me three minutes!"

Jessica and Vicky worked and traveled night and day for the next three days. At the end of that time they had located the spouses or parents of four of Bykov's guests who had been inexplicably out of contact for days. It was time to take what they'd gathered to Brad and Ving.

* * *

Brad and Ving were poring over the latest State Department Worldwide Travel advisory on one of the big screen monitors in the Comm Room when Vicky, Jessica, and Fly came to them. Jessica was carrying an accordion file roughly four inches thick. Ving glanced up in surprise as they entered.

"I thought y'all were on vacation," he teased.

"No, you did not! Brad knew exactly where we were, what we were doing, and he tells you everything." Vicky was mildly annoyed. The past three days had taken a grueling effort, and she was still not sure they had enough hard evidence to convince Brad to go ahead with an op even though they had a tentative bid for a retainer.

Brad switched off the monitor in front of him and pushed his chair back from the desk, swiveling it around to face the three women.

"So what have you got?"

"It's all here." Jessica handed him the thick accordion file. "It's quite a lot actually. There is no question that there is an ongoing ransoming operation at Khwām Sukh."

Brad didn't look up, he was leafing through each section of the file. "The place you two were talking about taking a vacation?"

"The very same." Now that she had seen what she considered hard evidence, she was impatient to get started. She knew what had to be done, and she knew Brad was going to balk at the concept. The trouble was, no matter how she considered it, there was no other way. She was going to have to infiltrate Khwām Sukh and do whatever it took to get Bykov to hold her for ransom. Otherwise Team

Dallas would never be able to find out where the Russian was holding the missing women, and Bykov would continue to extort the ultra-rich free from fear of reprisal.

Brad finished the documents in the accordion file with a grunt and handed it to Ving. He looked at Fly.

"Let me see the dossier on Bykov again." It was a command not a request. She could plainly see that he was not happy, so she didn't choose to remind him that it was okay to say "please" as she normally would have. Vicky clearly understood what was going to have to be done. Fly privately agreed with her, and she didn't want Brad any more irritated than he already was.

Brad read the dossier again, this time reading every word instead of skimming over it the way he had the first time. It took him almost an hour, and by then everyone in the room was fidgeting and nervous. He set the thick folder down on his desk.

Then he leaned back in his chair and laced his hands behind his head, thinking furiously as Ving reviewed the dossier. When Ving set the dossier down, Brad addressed no one in particular.

"Nobody has more sympathy for these women than I do, and I can tell you right now this sonofabitch Bykov should be terminated with extreme prejudice ... but that's not the business we are in. There is no way we can plan any kind of op without knowing where he's taking and holding these women. Hell, we don't even know whether he's taking them to anyplace in particular, they could be scattered around in different places around the Bay of Bengal. We couldn't even hijack that kind of satellite coverage if we knew when he was spiriting them out of ... what's this place's name ... Pleasures? All we know for sure is that he is transporting them out by chopper in the dead of night and that the flight time varies."

"We do know that the hostages are drugged," Jessica said quietly. "Rohypnol, from the descriptions given by the two women we interviewed who had actually been repatriated. Their estimate of the flight times could be wildly off."

"So could their descriptions of the torture chamber. Rohypnol induces short-term amnesia in most cases, and it would be easy to use a movie set made up to look like a dungeon."

"There are hundreds, if not thousands, of stone temples, monasteries, palaces, and tombs scattered around Thailand that wouldn't require much effort to make look like dungeons," Fly said. "The possibilities are endless. We need more to go on than that."

"What about the helicopter? Can't we get radar tracking on that? We know it's taking off from the resort…"

"No way, Ving. Even if I could hijack a satellite, which would be impossible because I don't know when he's taking a hostage out, even if I had it focused on the exact spot the chopper took off from, one sharp turn or evasive maneuver would take it out of the field of resolution and I couldn't change the attitude of the satellite fast enough to follow it. Besides, if it's flying nap of the earth, ground clutter would dirty up the image." Fly sounded frustrated. "I'd need eyes on it in a pursuit craft or a bug on the chopper."

Vicky sighed. She'd been dreading this moment for a couple of hours, ever since she'd come to the conclusion that she was going to go undercover on this one.

"Brad, we got an offer of a retainer, a substantial one, and there are innocent lives at stake. We've got to take this on."

"Vicky, we don't have any way of finding out where he's keeping them, we don't have a way of finding out where he is turning them back over to their families. We don't have anything we need to resolve this."

"Yes we do," she said, "we've got me."

"Say what?" Ving sat up suddenly in surprise and Brad's eyes narrowed.

"If you're thinking what I think you're thinking the answer is 'oh hell no,' Vicky!"

"Brad, there's no other way. I have to go inside Pleasures and convince that man to take me hostage for ransom."

# Chapter Thirteen

**Comm Room, Jacobs Ranchette**

After an hour or so of furious pacing around the corral, he cooled down enough to realize that no matter how much he hated the idea, Vicky was right. She was the only "in" they had to Bykov's scheme. *She's an experienced intelligence officer, and she's tough as hell. You know she can handle herself in combat, you've seen it yourself. If you hold her back because of your personal relationship you're going to destroy what you've got ... she'll think you don't believe she's capable of handling it. Face it, Brad, no matter what decision you come to, this one has to be done and you're going to pay for it in spades emotionally. The big difference is that if you don't take it, you're going to lose her for sure.* His mind made up, reluctantly, he walked back to the Comm Room.

* * *

"I'm going with her, Brad. End of story. You can either send me with her or I will buy my own ticket. One way or the other I will be there with Vicky."

Brad eyed his blonde cousin skeptically. "Jess, Vicky has experience undercover, this ain't her first rodeo. You are a hell of a combat trooper, I know that from experience. What you are not is the kind of siren that's going to attract Kirill Bykov's … err … attention."

*For God's sake, I have known her since the day she was born. How do I tell her she is not the seductress that Vicky is? How do I tell her it makes me uncomfortable enough that Vicky is going to have to let that bastard put his hands on her, that I can't send her into this viper pit with a clear conscience?*

"For one thing, you aren't rich enough. Bykov is only picking the richest of the rich."

*And, if Fly's dossier is to be believed, women who appeal to his prurient interests. I can't reconcile the mental image of my sweet little blonde cousin with the image of Vicky acting every bit the kind of vixen Bykov would lust after. He's far too refined and cultured to be the kind of guy turned on by an innocent virgin ... and yes, I know, since Charlie's been with the team the question of whether you're a virgin or not anymore is moot.*

"Vicky is not ultra-rich either," Jessica said hotly.

"Fly is making her a complete bogus background file, Jess. Besides, it's not the same. You are younger—"

"Whoa there, buddy," Vicky interjected. "I'm not *that* much older than her."

"I thought you'd be on my side in this, Vicky. She is younger than you are and she does not have your—" Brad struggled for the right word "—*experience* at manipulating men."

"Hey now!" Vicky didn't look particularly pleased with his implication.

"You diggin' that hole deeper, brother." Ving was having a hard time suppressing a smile. He had never seen Brad this flustered in all the years they had worked together—and they had been in some tight spots where the pucker factor had been tremendous.

"This is not a matter for debate, Brad; I'm going and that is that!"

Stunned, Brad met her gaze, but Jessica's never faltered. He had never seen her so determined, and she had never bucked him in front of any of the other team members before. Indecisiveness had never been a part of his character. Faced with his cousin's raw determination, he acceded to her demand—but he intended to have a private word with her later. A good leader never remonstrated with his subordinates in front of others. He reached down for a notepad and pen and began to scribble out the skeletal outline of an operation he was not fully confident was viable. He would give it his best shot, but inwardly he knew he would reserve his judgment as to whether the mission was a go or a no-go until the mission plan and op order were complete.

There was no way he was going to allow either Vicky or Jessica to infiltrate Pleasures Resort unless he was one hundred percent satisfied that he could keep them safe at all times. After he had sketched a broad outline of the mission plan, he intended to spend an hour or two with Fly Highsmith. He intended to have a long talk with her about her newest tech gadgets.

\* \* \*

"How sure are you of these things?" Brad held the tiniest of the drones on the tip of his index finger while he peered at it through a magnifying glass Fly had handed him for that purpose.

"If you're asking me if they're reliable, Brad, the answer is yes. Those tiny battery packs are good for twelve hours, and you can recharge them by exposing them to a regular light bulb for an hour.

You can fly one of them onto a shirt collar or even the back of a sleeve, and it will attach itself, clinging to the fabric. It will not withstand a blow of any kind, that's why I recommend attaching it to the back of the collar. Anytime the wearer is about to be scanned with detection devices, the operator can fly the drone into the air and away from the detector. Once the scan is over, the drone can be reattached.

"If you're asking me whether I have resolved the flight response issue yet the answer is … maybe. It's a matter of fine-tuning, more mechanical than electrical and that is very tough without the rest of my new equipment here."

"So how close do you think you are to finishing?"

"I can't really say. Brad, I'm working on this as hard as I can. If I was willing to let the intelligence community see how far I've come with these prototypes, I would fly to Fort Meade and use Rankin's lab. It's not a matter of me wanting to take credit for this, it's a matter of not trusting the higher-ups with them. I don't have a problem with them using my discoveries to spy on enemies, but I won't stand for them using the drones for political infighting and that's exactly what they would do with them. Not going to happen."

Brad was less concerned with politics than he was with the safety of Vicky and Jessica, but he understood Fly's objections ... and he knew she was right. If he tried to insist she would balk and there would be no chance of using the drones. He knew better than to issue an order that would not be obeyed. As far as Fly was concerned, the matter was closed.

"Thanks Fly, I appreciate your candor." He started to leave and then turned around. "Not trying to put any pressure on you, you understand, but the decision on whether to run this op hinges completely on whether you get those ready or not."

"Yeah," Fly muttered under her breath, "no pressure!"

\* \* \*

The outline of the mission plan, at least the skeleton of it, was spread out over several sheets from a legal pad. The entire team was clustered around a table in the Comm Center, contributing to the development of the op order.

Initially, the plan called for the team minus Fly, Vicky, and Jessica to arrive in Pattaya City on separate commercial flights three days before Vicky and Jessica were to arrive together at the spa. The team had split up, each member working on an annex to the operations order assigned based on their area of expertise.

\* \* \*

Jared Smoot was establishing a list of small arms and ordnance required. The first half of his list detailed their needs for a soft penetration of the resort itself. The team would necessarily remain covert on the island of Ko Phai. Brad's intention was that Bykov and his security force, however many men comprised it, remain totally unaware of the presence of Team Dallas. The weapons Jared selected had to be silent and effective. For sidearms he picked Ruger Mark Vs equipped with suppressors. The team SOP called for each individual to carry their own personal knives, but because they were infiltrating a friendly allied country, they would not be carrying any personal weapons with them. Everything would have to be obtained in country, but that was not Jared's problem. Charlie Dawkins would use his contacts in the enforcement arm of the Department of State to locate a supplier and set up delivery.

The second part of Jared's annex concerned the weapons needed to conduct a raid on whatever Bykov was using to house his hostages. The complete lack of intelligence regarding the size and type of force they would be facing and the type of facility they would be conducting the raid upon made the selection of the weapons and ordnance needed highly complicated. In the end Jared settled on the massive close-quarter firepower of the AA-12 fully automatic 12-gauge shotgun that Brad had recently tested. The weapon would be extremely difficult to acquire inside the United States, but it was available at a price on the black markets in Asia. The price would be high, but they would be worth the money. He didn't bother with larger caliber sidearms. The members of Team Dallas were all expert marksmen, and a well-placed .22LR cartridge was as effective as a .45 with the proper placement.

Ordnance was another matter. He needed a very powerful yet physically small high explosive that could be shaped into a directional charge and could generate a tremendous amount of heat. He finally chose Pentaerythritol tetranitrate (PETN). PETN is a powerful explosive material with a relative effectiveness factor of 1.66. The relative effectiveness factor conveys an explosive's power to that of TNT (Trinitritoluene), in units of the TNT equivalent in kilograms that would create the same explosive impact as one kilogram of TNT. PETN needed only six tenths the weight of explosive power to create the same destructive force as one kilogram of TNT. The explosive had to be plasticized in order to shape it, and it required a small quantity of another explosive as a detonator. Jared also included five pounds of C-4 and detonators in his list. It was relatively cheap and could be shaped as needed on site.

When he was satisfied that he had a complete list of the items needed for the op, he passed it to

Charlie, who promptly went to the secure phone in the Comm Center console and began to contact the people who would act as go-betweens in the black market purchases. They were all people he'd used before.

\* \* \*

Pete Sabrowski got on the horn with Herb Wilcox, the guy he had rented the Martin PBM-5 from in Jakarta on the mission to Borneo when Team Dallas had rescued William Darnell Duckworth IV, CEO of Duckworth International Petroleum. After a brief, cordial conversation, Pete set the landline handset down in its cradle and turned in his swivel chair to wait for a chance to get Brad's attention. It was several minutes before Brad glanced up from his desk to see Pete waiting expectantly.

"Yeah Pete, what's up?"

"I got a hold of Herb Wilcox in Jakarta; you remember, Tiny's brother?"

Brad acknowledged that he did with a nod of his head.

"He thinks he can locate me another Martin PBM-5, the twin of the one we used in Borneo and in just as good a shape. He says it's a little village on the coast of Burma, a few hundred air miles away from Bangkok."

"Sounds good, Pete."

Brad grinned. "Did you hear that, Jared? Add an RB-15 to your list, and make sure we get an outboard big enough to push it with a full load!"

"Roger that!"

Brad returned his attention to the yellow legal sheets scattered across the top of his desk. Placing his elbows on the table and resting his head in his hands, he concentrated hard.

*Where? Where the hell is he holding them? They are being transported by helicopter. Wonder what kind of bird Bykov has? Wait a minute! Satellite photos of the resort compound! I remember seeing the helipad on the photos Fly gave us but no chopper. I need to get her to check and see if there are any photos before or after the ones we got that will give us some kind of clue as to what kind of helicopter is flying in and out of this place!*

He speed dialed Fly's cell phone direct and told her what he wanted. Then he turned back to the details of the operation. *There's so damn much I don't know! We don't know where they're holding the hostages. We don't know the size of the opposition forces at the holding site or their armament. What the hell were you thinking, Jacobs? Taking on this op is insane and you ought to know better. Yeah, it is, but you know Vicky and Jessica. Those two hardheads are bound and determined to go ahead with this whether you commit Team Dallas or not, and there's no way you can let them go in without support. No way in hell.*

There was nothing else he could do. The planning had to go ahead. At this point all he could do was make sure the details of the operation covering the intel he already had were the best he was capable of devising.

## Chapter Fourteen

**Pattaya City, Thailand, present day.**

They came in separately on different flights; Qatar Airlines, Singapore Airlines, Bangkok Airways, and Air Asia. Willona had reserved two adjoining family suites at Varee Jomtien Beach on Jomtien Beach Road in Pattaya City, and all of them had taken shuttles from U-Tapao International Airport.

Jared Smoot, the last team member to arrive, drew a lot of attention as he walked through the lobby of the hotel. He was dressed as he normally dressed, that is to say he dressed like a Texan. Rawboned and whipcord thin, everyone in the lobby stared at his checkered shirt, leather vest, blue jeans, and boots. So many people had been staring at him at the airport that he had taken off his cowboy hat and carried it in his hand. *I didn't think this through. Seems like everybody in Thailand is in love with American Western movies, and so far all of them think I'm a movie star. Now everybody I've seen is gonna remember me.*

The desk clerk, a diminutive and extremely attractive young Thai woman, literally gushed as she welcomed him to the hotel and gave him the electronic key card to his suite. In fact, she insisted on accompanying the bellman and escorted him to his room, all the while staring up at him with adoring eyes. He'd also forgotten how far U.S. currency went in the Far East (except Japan, Japan was more expensive than New York City by a long shot). When he'd tipped the bellman with a ten-dollar bill, the man had almost cried with gratitude. The two hotel employees were so solicitous that he had to be almost rude to get them to leave him at the door.

Once inside, he found the suite empty and the door to the adjoining suite standing wide open. Brad and the other members of Team Dallas were gathered around a long conference table that Brad had ordered up to the suite from the concierge. All of them with the exception of Charlie Dawkins were drinking coffee from an urn placed strategically at the far end of the table. Charlie, who had just arrived from the airport in a shuttle with a broken air-conditioner, was opening a bottle of ice-cold Singha beer. Jared's throat was a little dry and he watched wistfully as Charlie tipped the bottle up to his lips and drank thirstily.

"Got another one a them?"

"Just one, Jared," Brad said. "We've got work to do and we need to be clear-headed." The warning was unnecessary, but Jared took no offense. Brad was in mission mode and he was always intense at the beginning of a mission.

"No problem, I just wanna wet my whistle."

Charlie crossed over to the refrigerator and removed another bottle of beer then tossed it to Jared who caught it one-handed and held up his free hand for the church key. Charlie flipped him the bottle opener and Jared caught it, moving it in one smooth motion to the bottle cap. Snapping the cap off, he drained the bottle.

Ving looked up at him. "You know this place ain't civilized, right?"

Jared flashed the massive black man a thin smile. "I'm guessin' that means they ain't no bacon on the room service menu."

"Kin ya b'lieve that? Uncivilized I tell ya! These people are inhuman! How they 'spect a man to live without bacon? It jist ain't right!"

Ignoring the byplay, Brad turned his attention to Charlie, who was savoring the last of his Thai beer. "You got an ETA on your point of contact?"

Charlie glanced down at his wristwatch. "I allowed three hours for travel delays. He should be here around sixteen hundred hours."

Brad grunted. "All right. Grab a shower, get a snack, get some shuteye and meet back here in my suite at fifteen forty-five hours. Remember—"

"Sleep can be a weapon," the rest of the team finished in unison. The phrase was one of Brad's hallmark sayings. He did not have to say it. Every man present, even Charlie Dawkins who had never been military, knew the truth of that trite phrase.

* * *

Kiet Benjawan was the third-generation scion of a Thai immigrant. Born in Los Angeles, he had attended Stanford University, where he had obtained a degree in political science. He had been hired by the Department of State the day he had graduated because of his facility with Far Eastern languages. He was fluent in Thai, Cambodian, Vietnamese, and Malay, while he was conversant in a half dozen other languages as well as English. The Department of State recognized early on the qualities essential for a deep cover operator and groomed him for the job. He was good at it. He had been assigned to Bangkok on his third operation and had proved so effective and fit in so well that he had remained there for several years. He'd had occasion to work with Charlie Dawkins twice during his career at State, and the two men had learned to trust each other implicitly.

When Charlie had contacted him this time, Kiet had responded to Charlie's request without question. Dealing in black market arms had stiff consequences in present day Thailand, but Kiet was well-established in the Bangkok underground. Surprisingly, the only items on Charlie's list that had been difficult to obtain were the RB-15 and the Mercury outboard. He had finally located the RB-15 in a warehouse in Vietnam, a leftover from a war that had ended forty-four years before. He'd been forced to substitute a Yamaha outboard for the Mercury. Mercury outboards were scarce and he could only find a couple of ancient ones for sale. If he'd had more time he could have ordered one, but the time constraints Jared had placed on the order made that impossible.

Two men from his crew had driven to Vietnam to collect the boat, and they had brought it back to the abandoned warehouse Kiet used as a headquarters for his own covert operations. Once it was safely inside, the boat had been unpacked, cleaned and inspected and then inflated to make sure it was still serviceable.

The entire order had been assembled and carefully packed into a nondescript 1980s-era Isuzu Bison truck with a hand-built metal cover over the bed. The truck was one Kiet had used before to smuggle arms and ammunition into Burma, Cambodia, Laos, and Vietnam. It appeared to be on its last legs, but beneath the rusted and battered metal skin the truck was pristine, and the motor was beefed up. The chase car he provided did not look as dilapidated as the truck, but it was just as reliable.

He checked the vehicles over personally before having his men cover both with canvas tarps, and then he returned to his office in the back of the warehouse to await the time he was expected to make the call to Charlie.

* * *

"The Garage Bar in fifteen," Charlie said, hanging up the room phone. "Don't need to go inside. He's sending a Volkswagen microbus to pick us up and take us to his warehouse." Brad and the others, clad in their tourist clothes, stood up and headed for the door.

"You know where this place is, right?"

"Yes I do, Brad. Kiet and I met there several times the last time I was here. It's maybe a five-minute walk from here."

The walk to the bar was actually a little disappointing to everyone but Charlie. Once they walked off the grounds of the hotel, the street they crossed, Jomtien Beach Road, looked pretty much like any street in any beach town along the Gulf Coast. The Garage Bar was a nondescript metal building about a block off the beach road with a canopy over the entrance that was covered with dried palm fronds intended (unsuccessfully) to imbue the business with a little tropical atmosphere.

Underneath the canopy there was a collection of bar girls that called out to them, trying to entice them inside. Before the men of Team Dallas could even bother to give them an appraising glance, a vehicle horn sounded behind them. As one they turned around to see a garishly painted VW microbus bearing down on them from the direction of the beach road. The driver was wearing a brightly colored tropical shirt and a big wide smile. He pulled up alongside them and called out through the passenger window.

"Greetings from Kiet!" He had recognized Charlie.

* * *

The warehouse was well to the east of the city in a cluster of heavily wooded hills. It was obvious from the rutted path leading up into the woods from the main road that there had been very little vehicular traffic on it. When the microbus approached the warehouse, Brad had a hard time believing that it was fit for human occupancy. The metal sheathing and roofing was rusted and dented, and in many places panels were missing entirely. The right front corner of the building was crumpled by the hanging roots of a 200-year-old banyan tree. A ficus tree was growing through a gap in the roof at the left front of the building caused by a missing roof panel. The entrance door was the size of the door on a two-car garage, but there was nothing visible through it.

The microbus pulled up to the entrance and the driver honked the horn (which sounded remarkably like beep-beep from the old roadrunner cartoons) and waited patiently. In a moment a large black canvas curtain opened, revealing lights and vehicles within. The curtain had camouflaged the entrance so effectively that it had fooled Brad and the rest of Team Dallas. The microbus drove inside and the curtain was closed behind them.

"Charlie!" A slim Asian man with coal-black hair and a Pistol Pete mustache approached the microbus with a huge smile on his face. Charlie was the first team member out of the VW, and he hurried to greet the Asian man with a brotherly embrace.

"Kiet! It's been a long time, brother!" Charlie's face was wreathed with a massive grin. He turned and beckoned for the rest of Team Dallas to exit the bus. Brad and the others filed out and approached the two men.

"Kiet, meet Team Dallas. This is Brad Jacobs, our boss, Mason Ving, Jared Smoot, and Pete Sabrowski." Kiet shook each man's hand as Charlie introduced them.

"I have to confess, I have heard of you before now. There is not a great deal of information available about you even in the intelligence community, but what there is speaks very highly of you. You are well thought of in the highest circles."

Brad looked slightly ill at ease. "I'm not sure I'm comfortable with those in the highest circles being aware of what I'm doing."

Kiet and Charlie both laughed. It was Kiet who responded. "There are only two people in my highest circle who I trusted to give me information about you, and you know them both. One of them is a very special lady named Felicity Highsmith. The other one is my blood brother standing right in front of you." He stuck out his hand again to Brad. "Welcome to Thailand."

Pete and Jared were already moving toward the Isuzu truck. Pete began to inspect the mechanicals with a critical eye while Jared climbed up into the covered bed and began to check the equipment.

"It's all there," Kiet called out. "Check off everything on your list and make sure it's all satisfactory."

"They are pros, Kiet. It's no reflection on you, they are just thorough professionals." Charlie grinned and clapped his old friend on the back. "You wouldn't happen to have a Singha on ice back in that office of yours would you? Only had time for one when I got to the hotel and I'm still thirsty!" He turned his head slightly to the side and winked at Brad, who nodded imperceptibly, confirming that he understood Charlie was going to keep his buddy occupied while the team finished carrying out their inspection of the equipment and vehicles.

"Sure do, Charlie. Let's go hoist one while your friends finish up here. We can catch up on old times." The two old friends wandered off into the dark recesses of the warehouse while Brad and Ving joined Pete and Jared.

"What do you think, Pete?"

"The outside of his truck looks like hell, Brad. The underside is another matter entirely. It looks for all the world like they jacked up the rust on this thing and drove a new truck under it. Looks like they beefed up the motor a little too."

"What about the car?"

"I wish I had one just like it back in the States. It's a nineteen eighty-three Toyota FJ43 Land Cruiser. The body is not in as bad a shape as the truck, but the mechanicals are pristine. Give me a week in a body shop and I could take this thing to a car show!"

Brad walked around the Land Cruiser noting the canvas roof and the seating for four. The tires were brand new but they had been muddied up, just like the ones on the truck so it was unlikely that anyone would notice unless they were right on top of the tires, and Brad had no intention of letting anyone get close to either of the vehicles. They would move out at full dark and take back roads and back streets to the waterfront warehouse that Willona had rented over the telephone three days before. She was shrewd and had insisted on extensive photographs of the inside and outside of the warehouse before she had signed the lease electronically, paying for three months in order to avoid suspicion.

"What about the equipment, Jared?"

"It's all here, Brad. The shotguns are absolutely perfect, brand new. Still got the cosmoline on 'em so we'll have to clean 'em when we get to the new warehouse. Explosives look good, they're all in brand-new packaging. The PETN is already plasticized, and the C-4 bricks are still in U.S. Army packaging. He gave us a choice ... we've got clackers and wire and we've got radio-controlled detonators for the C-4. All that's left for us to check is this RB-15." He grunted and there was the sound of a heavy object being dragged across the metal bed of the truck. Ving hopped up inside the covered bed to help him and immediately there was a loud thunk.

"Sheeit Jared! Ya coulda tol' me I couldn't stand up in here!"

There was a dry chuckle from inside the truck. "I woulda thought ya'd figger that out for ya'self!" The comments were followed by more dragging sounds and then the two men appeared at the back of the truck. They hopped down and Brad and Pete helped them lower the heavy rubber boat to the floor of the warehouse. Then Jared climbed back into the truck and reappeared a moment later with a battery-operated air pump.

Without asking, Pete took the long leads from the air pump and connected them to the battery terminals on the FJ43 while Jared hooked up the feeder hose to the first of the compartments in the nose of the boat. While Jared was busy inflating the boat, Brad climbed up into the back of the truck to check the AA-12 shotguns himself. As Jared had said, the guns still had their protective coating from the factory. Heavy canvas bags contained drum magazines for the shotguns and there were three cases of 12-gauge Remington shells. The shells were double-aught buckshot.

"Perfect! Jared, let Charlie ride shotgun on the truck with you when we move out. Pete, Ving, and I will bring up the rear in the chase car. As soon as we check out the warehouse, we need to load these magazines. I want to get everything ready before Pete leaves to pick up the aircraft."

"You plan on inflating the boat there at the warehouse?"

"Roger that. We've only got to carry it about one hundred and fifty meters to the water from there and we will be moving at night. For no more distance than that we can put the boat on top of the Land Cruiser and walk it over. That bastard is heavy enough even without the outboard. There's no way the four of us can tote it by hand."

"Yeah, that Yamaha is a heavy mother. Come to think of it, what are we gonna do with it after we board the aircraft? I didn't think of that," Jared replied.

Brad smiled. "It's not like you to miss a detail like that in an op order."

"Hey, we haven't done the whole op order yet. We worked on the annexes separately, and if you hadn't noticed, I was jumping through hoops trying to make sure I didn't leave anything out on the equipment list and working with Fly on her little flying gizmos."

"True. Pete specified a double door in the fuselage and the aircraft comes equipped with a manual winch. We'll just reel it in and secure her to the deck with cargo straps. At this point we can't rule out the possibility that we'll need her again."

\* \* \*

Per the plan, the two vehicles moved out as soon as it was full dark. Taking back roads into the city and then back streets over to the ramshackle waterfront warehouse at Dongtan Beach off Jongtien Beach Road, they moved unnoticed through the night traffic of Pattaya City.

Jared nosed the Isuzu right up to the sliding entrance door and Charlie hopped out to open it for him. Wasting no time, Jared drove the big vehicle inside, leaving enough room for the Land Cruiser to pull in behind him. Once both vehicles were inside Charlie quickly closed the entrance door.

"Jared, I'm going to find the lights and hit them. You do a quick recon outside and see how much light escapes. I don't want to draw any unnecessary attention to this building. I don't know how long it's been unoccupied, but I don't need any of the locals getting curious over the next three days." Brad removed a small but powerful tactical flashlight from the cargo pocket of his khaki jeans and turned it on then began a quick search for light switches. Using his small penlight, Jared located the back door to the warehouse and quietly slipped outside.

\* \* \*

Sunan Lamsam slowly raised the back of the driver's seat where he had been reclining for the last twenty-four hours as soon as he heard the vehicles pull up to the warehouse door. There were two of them; an old Isuzu Bison truck with a jerry-built metal cargo box built onto the bed and an old Land Cruiser. A man climbed out of the passenger side of the Isuzu and opened the warehouse door. The instant the door was opened, both vehicles drove inside. Curious.

His sources had informed him that a foreigner had rented the run-down building for an exorbitant amount and that had naturally aroused his curiosity. The sum mentioned had been sufficient to rent a brand-new climate-controlled facility in a much better part of town. That had aroused his curiosity even further. The battered gray eight-year-old Mitsubishi sedan was nondescript enough that it did not stand out, and it had barely made it, sputtering and smoking to the off-road vacant lot he had selected for his observation post. He had picked the spot because it offered the best view of the disreputable warehouse as well as the entrance. As best he could recollect, the former tenant had left the building in disgust without paying his back rent because the landlord had refused to make necessary repairs.

Lamsam never saw the shadowy figure that slipped around the back side of the warehouse.

\* \* \*

"We have eyes on us," Jared said quietly.

"How many?"

"Just the one, Brad. He didn't see me, and I couldn't get close enough to tell you anything about him. Just that he is sitting in the car staring at this warehouse."

"Could be anybody. Round everybody up and bring them over here."

The five of them formed a rough circle in front of the Isuzu. "All right, we're being watched. Let's hope he didn't get a headcount. I want the four of you to walk out the front door and padlock it behind you. I'm gonna stay with the gear, and I want the rest of you to catch a cab and head for the red light district. Charlie, you will know where that is."

"Sure. Most of the tourists go to Soi Cowboy, a lot of expatriates hang around there and there are more signs in English."

"Good. I want you running in and out of the bars and strip clubs, split up if you have to, but make sure you lose our observer. When you're sure you've lost him, make your way back here." Brad glanced down at his wristwatch. "I don't want to leave this gear unattended, so I'll stick around for now. You guys be back here by zero three hundred. We can make our way back to the hotel then as long as you manage not to get yourselves tailed." He softened his comment with a grin. Brad had complete confidence that these men were more than a match for any tail, regardless of the skill of the followers.

* * *

"Ya think I can find me some bacon in that Soi Cowboy place?"

"I don't know, Ving, maybe. I know a lot of ex-pats hang out there. I suppose there's someplace you can get an American breakfast."

"Then let's get a move on, Charlie! I'm *hongry* an' I ain't had me no bacon since we left Texas … y'all gotta know that ain't civilized!"

"I think we ought to take two cabs," Jared said so quietly that only the four of them could hear him. "I only saw one observer, and we can throw him off our trail right off the bat if we split up here." They were standing at the end of the rutted driveway at the edge of the side street leading to Jomtien Beach Road. "Charlie, you and Ving go to the Soi Cowboy district, the cabbie will know where to take you when you tell them that. Me an' Pete will go over to Patpong an' check out a few of the clubs there."

Charlie looked up in surprise. "I didn't think you'd ever been to Thailand before. How'd you know about Patpong?"

Jared gave him a sly grin. "I got friends, Charlie, an' ain't none a them monks."

Charlie called for two cabs and within fifteen minutes all four men were headed for Bangkok's premier pleasure districts.

* * *

Jared was the first one back to the warehouse three minutes before 0300 hrs. He glanced over at the gray sedan in the vacant lot and could not see anyone inside. Curious, he approached it cautiously, but when he reached the car, it was empty. Noiselessly he moved to the front door of the warehouse and checked the padlock. It was undisturbed. His gut told him that something was wrong even though everything appeared to be in order. Weaponless, he remembered seeing a stack of leftover rebar outside the rear door of the warehouse earlier.

Silently, he lifted a short piece of reinforcing steel bar left over from some long ago concrete. As quietly as he could, he slipped the lock on the back door of the warehouse and stepped inside. The only light in the warehouse was from a single bulb suspended over a shabby steel desk in what had once been an office of some kind. Jared remembered having seen several tattered ancient posters of scantily dressed females gracing the walls earlier. Hearing the low murmur of voices coming from the office, he moved silently on the balls of his feet, rebar at the ready.

"You must be gettin' old, Jared," he heard Brad call out. "I heard ya when you came in the back door. Come on in and meet our new friend."

Jared let the short steel rod drop to his thigh and walked into the office. Sitting in a pool of light cast by the lone bulb sat Brad and a slender Asian man dressed in a Hawaiian shirt and khaki cargo shorts.

"Jared Smoot, meet Inspector Sunan Lamsam of the Special Branch, Royal Thai Police."

# Chapter Fifteen

**Pleasures Resort, Ko Phai Island, present day.**

The only limousine on the island rolled up to the entrance of the resort and was passed through the gate. It rolled around to the main entrance and the chauffeur remained at the wheel as two uniformed bellmen came outside. One opened the rear door while the other went to the trunk. A moment later, a uniformed boy pushed a brass cart out and began to unload luggage.

The first passenger out of the limo was a stunning, leggy redhead in an eye-popping emerald green silk pants suit straight from the couture houses in Milan. It fit her slender figure to perfection, and she wore no blouse beneath the blazer, which displayed tantalizing glimpses of the tanned and unfettered breasts beneath it. An elegant gold pendant set with a large emerald dangled between her breasts, calling even more attention to the smooth, creamy cleavage so fetchingly displayed.

The second passenger to emerge from the limousine was a younger but equally spectacular blonde with an athletic build. The younger woman was wearing a less revealing ensemble that nevertheless accentuated the perfection of her body. The bellman who held the door for them greeted them effusively and politely and then ushered them inside the main entrance. Neither woman checked to see about their luggage. They knew it would be delivered to their respective suites, it was clear they were used to being treated like royalty.

Mai greeted them in the foyer and personally escorted them to their suites. No waiting for these two. Bykov observed their entry with interest from the console on his office desk. He watched the redhead with particular interest. Aside from the fact that Mikhail's detailed dossier on the woman revealed that her husband was an extraordinarily wealthy oil magnate in Dallas, it also hinted that she had particularly fascinating prurient interests of a nature that Bykov found irresistible.

Bykov watched the redhead as she moved from the field of vision of one security camera to the next all the way to the entrance to her suite. For the time being, his focus was on the redhead. He would check in on the blonde later. He spared a single second to glance down at her dossier. Victoria Chance Timmons, an ordinary name for an extraordinary woman. Movement in the woman's suite drew his eyes back to the monitor. He isolated the feed from the pin cameras in her suite and enlarged them until they filled the big screen of one monitor. His eyes widened as she unfastened the buttons on her blazer and tossed the expensive garment casually onto the bed.

* * *

The technicians who'd installed the pin cameras in the suite had been highly professional, but Vicky's practiced eye had spotted the one in the bedroom the moment she arrived there. She smiled to herself and fingered the emerald pendant between her breasts, switching off the tiny drone perched on the collar of her blazer, and then removed the blazer. She tossed it onto the bed, careful not to dislodge the drone. There were some things she was going to have to do on this operation that she had no wish for the rest of the team to watch.

Her relationship with Brad Jacobs was new territory for her. She had never felt about any man the way she felt about Brad. Unquestionably the relationship was no dalliance, and there was no doubt that she loved him. As to whether or not it was a lifetime commitment she couldn't be certain yet. There was a salacious side to her personality that reveled in the exhibitionistic role she was going to have to play to ensure that Bykov would take her as one of his hostages. Brad had only seen a little of that side of her when they had first met in Cabo San Lucas. They had discussed the nature of this operation privately, but neither of them had been specific about boundaries, deliberately skirting the issue. Brad might have had some in mind, but Vicky was determined to succeed and she was not about to let false modesty impede her. If it required a little slap and tickle with Bykov to lure him into doing what she wanted, so be it. She was up for it—and to tell the truth, she was more than a little turned on by the prospect.

*This room is everything the brochure promised and more. The furnishings are exquisite and the colors are magnificent! That bed! Big enough for a playground ... not that I intend to bring anybody in here. I doubt Bykov ever visits the guest rooms anyway. From everything I read and everything Fly told me, the man is a serious womanizer, and I would bet my last dollar that he has a love nest somewhere around here and probably not at the resort. I'm safe enough in here, no doubt about it ...*

*so I think I'll start our little pavane right here and now.*

Making a half turn as if she were checking out the bedroom, Vicky lifted her hands and ran them through her hair. Knowing she was being watched excited her, and her pink nipples rose into hard little knots. She segued into a stretch, thrusting her chest forward and tightening the hard, flat muscles of her belly, luxuriating in the thrill of knowing Bykov was watching her. Kicking off her four-inch heels, she dropped her hands to the front of her pants, unfastened the button and slid the zipper down before wriggling out of them. She raised one slender leg and booted the emerald green pants up onto the bed beside the matching blazer. Wearing only a pale green thong, she strode over to the bathroom door. Framed in the doorway, she turned back and stared in the general direction of the camera. Then she hooked her thumbs into the thong and thrust it down to her ankles. Stepping out of the flimsy scrap of cloth, she stepped into the bathroom and turned the shower on.

It took only a few seconds to spot the pen camera concealed in the crown molding of the ceiling. Vicky smiled inwardly and reached for the soap. Showtime!

\* \* \*

Jessica was thoroughly impressed with her suite. Remembering all of Vicky's advice, she checked out every feature of the room, uttering little noises of delight as she did so. She did not locate any of the cameras, they were too well concealed for her inexperienced eye. Knowing she was being watched, she forced herself to strip down to bra and panties and then slipped on the monogrammed terry cloth robe provided by the resort. Only then did she remove her undergarments and head for the bathroom. Surely she would be allowed that much privacy. Jessica closed the door behind her and then stepped behind the opaque glass door in the overlarge shower before removing the robe. Turning on the water as hot as she could stand it, she began to lather up and scrub off the grime of the long Transpacific flight.

She was definitely suffering from jet lag, but Vicky had insisted they clean up and then meet by the pool. Jessica really didn't mind. A nice tropical drink, perhaps followed by a massage from one of the muscle-bound studs from the brochure sounded like a good way to end her day. There was no doubt in her mind that she loved Charlie, but there was no way she was going to pass up a great massage from a hot-looking guy. No way in hell.

* * *

Bykov watched the redhead, his eyes glued to the monitor as she sashayed around the suite in the nude. Magnificent! The woman had to be part feline. She preened and stretched, displaying an incredible body as if it was a piece of erotic art.

Bykov's hand went to the front of his trousers to adjust himself. It wouldn't do for Mikhail to notice his arousal, he had to appear aloof and unaffected. The redhead stirred him ... Timmons, her name was. Victoria Timmons. Unquestionably this one was a candidate for his personal harem. Unless he was sadly mistaken, and he rarely was, Victoria Chance Timmons was a wildcat in bed. He suspected it would take all his wiles to seduce her, and that was okay. It would be a challenge, and he thrived on challenges. Patience would be the key with this one.

\* \* \*

Vicky knocked on the door adjoining her room to Jessica's. Jessica answered almost immediately. She was wearing the monogrammed terry cloth robe, but hers, unlike Vicky's, was closed and belted. Vicky's hung open in front, the belt ends dangling down to the hemline. Jessica's jaw dropped. The garment Vicky was wearing, a microkini, covered nothing and revealed everything.

"My God, Vicky, you'd just as well go naked!"

"That's the idea, Jess," Vicky said dryly. Then she leaned forward into the door frame, where she was certain there was no pin camera, touching her lips with her forefinger and shaking her head no. She straightened up, her hand at her side and took a half step back.

"It doesn't hurt to let them look, dear. You just have to draw the line at being touched. Nobody lays a hand on this body unless I say so, you know that. Come on, let's get to the pool. I can hear a tall, thin flute of champagne calling my name!"

The two women linked arms and marched out the front door of Vicky's suite. They engaged in meaningless chatter, their heads together conspiratorially, occasionally breaking into gales of laughter. When they reached the poolside, they were welcomed by an incredibly handsome man with a muscular body and rugged good looks. He looked like he could've been a movie star in an action adventure movie. Dressed in what appeared to be a white Roman toga with gold facing around the hem, his broad manly chest was covered in tight black curls that Jessica instinctively wanted to brush her fingers through. His bronzed skin was gleaming with a light sheen of suntan oil that smelled of coconuts.

"Good afternoon, ladies!" He smiled broadly, exposing even white teeth that could have graced the poster in a dentist's office. He obviously knew who they were, because he led them to two chaise lounges bearing their suite designations in small discreet numbers. Vicky slipped off her robe and draped it over her arm. No sooner had he seated them than another man in an identical toga rolled over a small cart holding an open bottle of champagne on ice and two elegant crystal flutes. A tray laden with bite-sized canapés and fresh cut fruit was on the cart as well. The man, just as gorgeous as the first one, lifted a silver cover off of another tray bearing a selection of cheeses and dainty crackers. "Compliments of the resort, ladies."

The man who had brought the cart made a half bow and walked away. The first man flashed them another broad grin. "My name is Jason, ladies, and I am your server today. If there is anything you want, simply beckon me and I will provide you with *anything* you desire." He had been nothing less than respectful and courteous, yet his emphasis on the word "anything" and the twinkle in his eyes when he said it left no doubt in either woman's mind that he was accustomed to providing even the most intimate of services to the guests. He gave a half bow and backed away just as the first man had, but his flashing blue eyes never left off visually caressing every curve and fold of Vicky's body.

"Is it safe to talk out here?" Jessica asked nervously, scrutinizing their surroundings for microphones or listening devices.

Vicky leaned back in her chaise and raised her arms, locking her fingers on her head and incidentally thrusting her proud breasts forward and allowed her eyes to inspect everything around her before she answered. "I think so, but keep it low-key. Don't say anything obvious." She spoke in such a low voice that she was barely audible over the sounds from the pool area.

"He looked like he wanted to eat you alive," Jessica murmured with a chuckle.

"I wouldn't be surprised. Take a look around us, Jess. I expect he gets plenty of offers from these heifers every day."

"He wasn't looking at me, Vicky. He only had eyes for you." Jessica did not know whether to feel amused or insulted, but she was good-natured and went for amused. "From the looks of the clientele, they must feed these guys raw testosterone."

It was Vicky's turn to chuckle. "What did you expect? Ladies only and the wait staff is one hundred percent prime beefcake. Clearly this place is designed to stroke the libido of every single guest."

"Well, don't tell Charlie, but mine just kicked into overdrive."

"If you remembered to bring your little friend, Jess," Vicky said, referring to Fly's micro drone, "you just did."

"Oh shit!" Jessica blushed bright crimson and covered her mouth with her hand.

"Never mind, Jess. Just drink your champagne and let's nibble a few of these canapés."

\* \* \*

After choosing to forgo a massage at the spa, Vicky and Jessica returned to their suites. When they arrived, they found complimentary gift baskets filled with bottles of wine and select chocolates. The baskets were garnished with colorful, delicate tropical flowers. There were notes on heavy paper cards embossed with the Khwām Sūkh logo. Each was addressed to them by name, welcoming them to the spa and suggesting that it might be nice if they could find the time to dine with him at some point during their stay. They were signed, "Kirill Bykov."

# Chapter Sixteen

**Pattaya City, three days before Vicky and Jessica arrive on Ko Phai Island.**

"I'm gonna take it as a good sign that he ain't hauled us all off to the pokey." Ving sipped from the familiar red-and-white can of a ubiquitous American soda. As much as he would've enjoyed a beer, he was far too full of the bacon he had found in an all-night eatery in the Soi Cowboy red light district of Bangkok after he and Charlie split up. Much to his displeasure, he discovered that the incredibly cheap prices in Bangkok did not extend to such staples as American bacon. Satisfying his craving had proved monstrously expensive, but he had indulged himself anyway. The proprietor of the eatery had been forced to hurry out to a farmers' market in the district, which was open all night like every other business on the street, to purchase a cut of pork that he could slice up and pass off as bacon. He had paid a premium for the meat and had, of course, passed the premium on to Ving, with a huge markup for himself for his trouble.

"We're not out of the woods yet," Brad said sourly. "The guy likes us, he's a retired Marine, a Royal Thai Marine, and he spent his whole time in service in their equivalent of Force Recon. Different uniforms but still a Marine. Brothers in arms, and that's thicker than blood."

"Yeah, but he's an inspector with the Royal Thai Police, Brad, and it's his job to catch people like us and deport us—or, worse, haul us off to Bang Kwang Central Prison—and believe me, all the horror stories you heard about Far Eastern prisons pale into insignificance compared to the realities of Bang Kwang."

"Bad place, huh?" Pete asked in a morose voice.

"It's their equivalent of death row. It's overcrowded, lice infested, and the prisoners are kept on starvation rations—not so much because the Thais are cruel but because with the overcrowding their budget is not big enough to feed them all properly."

Ving grunted. "The strongest eat and the rest do without."

"If they're lucky. The men on death row here have no hope. No appeal, no chance of getting out. And none of them have long to live. They have nothing to lose by killing another inmate for some extra food."

"Don't give up yet, Charlie. The bond between Marines of any nation is far stronger than you imagine. I told you, he likes us, and he is highly pissed about Bykov running a ransom operation in his district without his ever having caught a whisper of it. If he goes to his superiors and has to tell them that we are the ones who uncovered Bykov's illegal operation in his area of responsibility he's gonna have egg on his face … big time. I made him a proposition, and I hope he's gonna go for it. Be patient and let's see what happens." Brad glanced toward the office with its single ancient light bulb where Inspector Sunan Lamsam was speaking quietly into his cell phone.

"I hope he does," Charlie said nervously.

"Maybe you should give your buddy Kiet a call and see if he has a back door into the Royal Thai Police…"

Charlie looked stunned, as if he'd been struck by a bolt of lightning. "I never thought of that." He fumbled in his pocket for his cell phone and then punched in an international number from memory.

\* \* \*

"Sir, I must respectfully request a little leeway here…" Lamsam was sweating. The chief inspector was a hardass, a stickler for the rules, and he hated any deviation from them.

"Yes sir!" He felt as if he were being drawn over a bed of hot coals. The phone conversation with the chief inspector had dragged on for over an hour, ever since the American Marine had startled him by admitting that he and his team were in Thailand to put a stop to an outrageous ransoming operation being carried out under his very nose. He'd felt a strange but strong kinship to the sandy-haired American, not least because of their shared experiences as Marines in the service of their respective countries. The bonds of brothers in arms was an old and honorable one, universally recognized even by former adversaries. In Brad Jacobs' case, it was a matter between two allied forces, an even closer bond. Jacobs had come across as a true leader, a man to be respected … and as the team members had returned, Lamsam had noted the respect he was accorded by his subordinates.

The problem was twofold. First, there were the two vehicles loaded down with enough arms and ordnance to start a small war sitting in the warehouse—a major criminal infraction sufficient to send the whole team to Bang Kwang forever. Foreigners with weapons and explosives were treated harshly in Thailand and rightly so.

The second problem was that these men were *Marines,* men who had fought and bled for their country. Honorable men who had come to *his* country to right something *he* was bound by oaths to right ... it was a big part of his responsibility to do what they were trying to do. They intended to stop a crime by committing a crime, and that was something Lamsam would have found completely intolerable had they not been honorable men. It had been this quandary that had driven him to seek guidance from the chief inspector, and it had been his deep conviction of Jacobs' honorable character and intentions that had kept him from revealing the details to the head of Special Branch and pleading for a little latitude in dealing with the problems.

He was surprised when the chief inspector placed his call on hold and left him waiting for such a long time. The battery on his cell phone was getting low, and he was fearful that one of the Quick Reaction teams had been dispatched to the warehouse to take both him and the Americans into custody. His phone, after all, carried a GPS transmitter. The chief inspector could easily have pinpointed his location.

When the chief inspector came back on the line, Lamsam listened open-mouthed with shock as he received his instructions. The last thing the chief said to him was mind-numbing. "Lamsam, I'm washing my hands of this entire matter. Go ahead and do what you think is best. If you are successful, I will be first to commend you. If you should fail, you'll be on your own. I won't interfere, but you'll get no help from this office. Understood?"

"Yes sir!" The line went dead, leaving Lamsam with a stupefied look on his face as he stared at the chunk of hard plastic in his hand. It was a long time before he stood up and went out to speak with the Americans.

* * *

"What was that all about?" Ving asked, all traces of his homespun Louisiana accent and colloquial speech gone.

"Looks like Charlie's phone call paid off." Brad breathed a sigh of relief when Lamsam went out the back door of the warehouse. "But we aren't completely out of the woods yet."

"I'm uncomfortable with those 'conditions' he mentioned."

"Whatever they are, Charlie, we're going to have to abide by them. He's got us by the short and curlies." Brad rubbed his chin thoughtfully.

"If I don't get out of here this morning we're never going to get the aircraft in time and that's gonna screw the whole op, Brad."

"I know, Pete, but I gave him my word we wouldn't leave here until he gets back."

"Brad," Charlie said hoarsely, "Jessica and Vicky…"

"They won't be landing at U-Tapao until tomorrow afternoon. I can get hold of them in flight if I have to. I wouldn't leave either of them in jeopardy, Charlie, you know that."

"So, what, we just wait for Lamsam?" Charlie was frustrated and it showed.

"Give him a couple of hours, Charlie. He's an honest cop and this is hard as hell for him. Sure, we need to get moving—especially Pete—but we can spare a couple of hours. His boss laid one hell of a burden on him a little bit ago, and if you look at it objectively, *we* have put him in a position where he has to decide whether to risk his whole career to help us. I can only hope he's as pissed at Bykov as he says he is."

"Yeah, hope," Ving said evenly. "Wouldn't be no question about what your decision would be in the same situation, Brad." No one else had a comment.

\* \* \*

Sunan Lamsam forced his hands to stop trembling. The magnitude of the decision he was faced with shook him to his core. The chief inspector had given him the latitude he asked for but at the same time given him enough rope to hang himself. Exposing Bykov and bringing him to justice would be the crown jewel in his Special Branch career—but not if these American Marines got credit for breaking the case. Brad Jacobs was a man to inspire respect. Sunan Lamsam considered himself to be a sterling judge of character, and from his observations of Team Dallas, he was convinced that these men were formidable.

Their lack of specific intelligence regarding numbers and armaments of their opposition troubled him, but the awesome firepower packed in the two vehicles inside the warehouse should be enough to handle anything short of an army. Still, the prospect of failure loomed over the entire operation and the chief inspector had been brutally clear about the consequences of failure. Should the operation go south, Lamsam would most certainly be drummed out of Special Branch and probably imprisoned for violating the laws concerning foreigners with weapons on Thai soil. He and all his generations would be dishonored.

A phrase often repeated by his grandfather, a former chief inspector himself, kept running through Lamsam's mind. "*Mìmī xarị thî̀ klâ thả mìmī xarị dî̂ rạb*" (nothing ventured, nothing gained). It was an enormous gamble, but if he insisted Jacobs and his team take him along on the operation, he could find a way to take credit for the investigation and the bust—and that made the risk acceptable. A case this big rarely came along, even in Bangkok. If the stars were aligned in his favor, he might be able to pull this off before blood was shed.

He raised his eyes to the heavens, praying to his ancestors that he was doing the right thing, and then walked back inside the warehouse to face Brad Jacobs and Team Dallas.

* * *

They made it to the beach with no mishaps. Pete was in Vietnam collecting the Martin PBM-5, but Lamsam took his place. He had insisted on participating in the op as a condition for not simply turning them over to the Royal Thai Police. Seeing no other options, Brad had accepted, although he was not pleased. It was Ving who pointed out that there might be a silver lining in this particular cloud.

"Ain't no tellin' where we gotta go from that island, Brad. It might just be handy to have a Thai cop along for the ride."

"I don't know, Ving. He's a cop first. I don't need him balking at the last second if we have to engage … he is going to do whatever he has to in order to avoid shedding blood. I don't want his hesitation to get one of us hurt or killed."

"He was a Marine, Brad. One of us," Ving had said simply.

The moon was full as they carried the boat into the surf. It took two of them to manhandle the outboard from the Land Cruiser out and attach it to the sternboard, and Charlie drove the vehicle back to the warehouse and locked it inside before returning to the beach and wading out to the waiting RB-15. Vicky and Jessica would be arriving the next afternoon, and the team would be in place when they got there. Lamsam had agreed to arrange for additional cover details for them through one of his CIs (confidential informants). Ving had been right; it was convenient to have the Thai cop along.

\* \* \*

"It would be better to skirt Ko Lan Island," Lamsan said above the throaty roar of the Yamaha outboard. "No one is likely to spot us from there. The current between Ko Lan and Ko Phai is surprisingly strong." The swells in the Bay of Bangkok were low and choppy, as was to be expected in such shallow water. The full moon was worrisome, but the shrimp trawlers that plied the bay were up north and west of the city of Bangkok, where the boat traffic was lighter and the population was less dense. Their primary concern was the patrol boats of the Royal Thai Navy.

## Chapter Seventeen

**Bay of Bangkok, one day prior to the arrival of Vicky and Jessica.**

Ko Phai was relatively uninhabited except by the staff and guests of Khwām Sukh, but Bykov had roving patrols and electronic surveillance devices that only covered the beach areas as most of the shoreline was rocky cliffs.

Lamsam pointed to one of the scalable cliffs and Jared throttled back the Yamaha outboard and guided the RB-15 nose in to the rock-strewn shoreline. He left the throttle on idle until Brad, Ving, Charlie, and Lamsam climbed out of the boat and grabbed hold of the gunnel ropes, and half lifted, half dragged the boat up onto the steep shoreline at the base of the cliff. Ving tilted the propeller shaft back with his hands so that it wouldn't drag on the rocks, the huge muscles of his arms standing out with the effort. In no time they had the boat covered with camouflage netting to conceal it from the prying eyes of the roving patrol boats of the Royal Thai Navy.

"Ya gotta be kiddin' me," Ving said, staring up at the cliff above them. "I hate climbin', Brad, ya know that." He was teasing. Brad had seen the big man scale an inverted cliff like a scared monkey once in Iraq, a cliff that would have challenged an Olympian. Ving was already unlimbering the one-hundred-twenty-foot length of climbing rope he had hooked to his belt with a D-ring. The incline was not as steep as it had first appeared, and the team had remarkably little trouble scaling it.

Once they had reached the summit, Brad gave the signal to move out, pointing at Lamsan to lead them. Jared, the team's point man, shadowed the Thai closely, more to observe Lamsam's technique than because of mistrust. As good as he was, and Jared Smoot was one of the best in the world, he never missed an opportunity to learn, and Lamsam was on his home ground.

Still dressed in civilian clothes and armed only with the suppressed Ruger Mark Vs and the hunting knives Jared had procured, they moved out single file, like ducks in a row so they could move more quickly through the underbrush. Lamsam led them through the tropical forest to a ridge running down the center of the island that rose to an elevation of one hundred and fifty meters above sea level. Once over the ridge, Lamsam turned northward toward the resort. They marched silently for a few hundred meters until they came to a clearing dotted with a handful of rough thatched huts around a communal central campfire.

A solitary islander sat beside the fire on a section of rough-sawn log, sipping Mekhong Whisky from a battered tin cup. When the islander spotted them coming from the forest, he set his cup down and rose to greet Lamsam, whom he was expecting. Lamsam spoke with him briefly, and then the islander, wordlessly, led Team Dallas to a single hut somewhat larger than the rest and set at the far outside edge of the clearing.

The inside of the hut was primitively furnished with lashed together split bamboo furniture and lit by a single kerosene lamp.

"This is home for however long we have to wait," Lamsam said quietly. "Sleeping mats have been provided and they're rolled up over there in the corner. Chakan here, or his woman, will provide morning and evening meals as needed. He has been my informant here on the island for many years, and I prize his reliability." Lamsam spoke eloquently and articulately, as do many people who have studied English as a second language. His grammar and sentence structure were those of an English teacher in a public school. Chakan spoke to Lamsan in rapid-fire singsong Thai.

"*Teūxn phwk k̄heā kel̀yw kạb kār lādtrawen t̀hxngthel̀yw yìng khuṇ xyù̄ kıÎKhwāmŚuk̄hyìng yæ̀ thèā h̄ịr̀*" The lined, weathered face of the old islander looked strained in the flickering light of the kerosene lamp. He turned and made for the door to the hut.

"What was that all about?" Brad asked.

"He said the patrols near the resort are very active." Lamsam looked concerned.

"You said earlier they were just two-man patrols, right?"

"Yes, that's what he said initially."

"Then we've got it covered. Not to worry." Brad turned to survey the inside of the hut.

"Don't look none too homey," Ving drawled, "but I reckon I've slept in worse."

"Better than that bombed-out rubble we had in Fallujah."

"Ya jist had ta dredge that memory up, didn't ya, Brad?"

"It was pretty lousy…"

"Yeah, an' there ain't no hostiles tryin' ta blow us ta hell either so it's got that goin' for it."

Jared, who had once lain unmoving for forty-six hours in a honey pit to avoid capture by a band of seriously irate Al-Qaeda jihadists, made no remark at the conversation between Brad and Ving. He knew very well that both men were aware of the occupational hazards of a Force Recon sniper.

To his surprise, Lamsam felt camaraderie with these men who had obviously shared so many of the same experiences he had endured as a Marine. He had observed their movements on the march here and the way they worked together without needing more than hand signals. Their actions in danger areas had been automatic and efficient with no wasted effort. He'd been thoroughly impressed with their professionalism. He'd been fascinated with their familiarity with the weapons they had unloaded from the Isuzu while they were back in the warehouse, and he'd been amazed as he'd watched the one called Jared carefully form the PETN into several shape charges capable of blowing a hole in a three-foot-thick stone wall.

Lamsam broke into the casual banter between the friends.

"So tell me again, Brad. When we find out where Bykov is holding his victims, you said we'd take the boat out to the flying boat your man Pete is flying in from Vietnam. Your assault weapons are in Pattaya City, so how and when are you going to get them out to the aircraft?"

"As soon as Pete lets us know he is three hours out, I'm sending Jared and Ving back to collect the weapons and ordnance. Once Vicky and Jessica are on the move, I won't need them here anymore. They will take the gear out to Pete and load them on the bird."

"So how will we get out to the aircraft?"

"One of the guys will come back to pick you and me up at the creek mouth where we landed tonight and take us out to the bird."

"And the boat? What will we do with that, abandon it?"

"No way! We may need it wherever we're going. There's a winch aboard the aircraft and we're taking the boat on board when you and I get out there."

Lamsam mulled over the plan for a moment. "That sounds complicated. We were taught in the Royal Marines an acronym I believe you are familiar with … KISS."

"Keep it simple stupid." Ving laughed.

"Exactly. Your plan doesn't take into consideration a number of possibilities that come to mind."

Brad looked directly into the Thai's brown eyes. "We were faced with circumstances that forced us to come up with a plan with built-in flexibilities. That's something our Marines are intimately acquainted with. We call it 'Murphy's Law' and it affects every military operation I've ever been involved in."

"Murphy's Law? I don't believe I've ever heard of that."

""Anything that can go wrong will go wrong," Ving broke in again with a smile.

\* \* \*

Jared, being the lead reconnaissance man on Team Dallas, was the first of them to penetrate all the way to Pleasures. Creeping through the forest, he froze twice when he encountered separate two-man patrols. He did not get as close a look at the first patrol because they passed so close to him that he had to conceal his face behind a large stone on the forest floor. The men were conversing in a language that Jared recognized as Chinese, though he didn't speak more than a phrase or two in Mandarin. When the first patrol passed on by, Jared looked up to see that they had been following a footpath worn by the traffic of many feet over a period of time.

*I'm sure that was Chinese they were speakin'. This footpath tells me these guys follow a rigid routine. Good for me, not so good for them. I ain't gonna bet my life on it, but I'd bet money the other patrols do the same thing. I saw Chinese troops in Iraq, even though those bastards at G2 told me I was mistaken. Mistaken my ass. Those guys had PLA written all over 'em, Chinese Special Forces. That intel shoulda been spread out to the whole Expeditionary Force, but politics has infected even the Corps. The political weenies suppressed it, an' we sure paid the price for that, didn't we? It mattered to the guys that got killed, an' it mattered to me. I learned something from it though. Those Chinese SF types are real badasses. Tough as hell an' just as mean, but, just like the Nazis in World War II, they got a flaw. They don't have the ability to think on their own. If they don't have somebody to tell 'em what to do they're lost.*

Having learned from his first encounter, Jared kept his eyes open for another footpath. He ignored a couple of small game trails, no boot prints in those, but about another hundred meters closer to the resort he found another, broader path clearly marked with boot prints. He shook his head.

When he got within sight of the resort, he had trouble seeing over the walls. He spotted a gnarled banyan tree with thick foliage thirty meters to his left, and he crawled on his belly over to the thick and twisted aerial prop roots. He crawled around until the trunk was between him and the resort and then shimmied up the trunk until he could hide himself in the leaves. When he was near the top, he peered out at the resort, and what he saw there made him want to climb down immediately and go tell Brad ... but he was far too self-disciplined for that. He spent the next hour and a half observing activities within the resort, even though it had started to rain heavily, and then quietly made his way back to Chakan's hut to disseminate what he had learned when the lightning started.

* * *

Ving grimaced as the raindrops began to pelt down on him, fat raindrops as big as the end of his thumb. It was not his personal discomfort disturbing him, it was the fact that the rain was obliterating the track he was following. Within minutes the downpour made it impossible to tell a game trail from one made by men in boots ... and the roar of the rain drumming on the leaves, trees, and the ground was so loud that he couldn't hear anything else. He dropped to one knee and turned to scan the area for any sign of Brad. They had left Chakan's hut at the same time Jared had, and they had split up, looking for sign of the patrols both Lamsam and Chakan had mentioned. If they were to get close enough to the resort to monitor the micro drones Vick and Jessica were carrying, it was imperative that they get a feel for the routes followed by the patrols, the speed they traveled at, and their habits, good and bad, as they performed their duties.

From long experience, Ving knew that men tended to get complacent and lackadaisical when they performed repetitive tasks. He was looking for signs that would indicate carelessness or other lapses in discipline he could exploit to his advantage. It was his own letdown that nearly caused his undoing. As he turned to look for Brad, he felt a massive blow on his back that knocked him flat on his face.

*"Bié dòng nǐ shì shéi? Nǐ zài zhèlǐ zuò shénme?"*

The words were singsong, but he'd heard enough Thai, Korean, and Vietnamese to know the language was none of those. *Chinese?* Before he had time to think about it further, his instinctive reactions took over. As the heavy tread of a boot pressed down on the back of his neck, Ving spun onto his back, his ham-sized hand clamping on the toe of the boot, twisting it sharply, causing its wearer to yelp in pain and fall to the ground. Catlike, Ving didn't let up, pouncing on the fallen man, pinning his arms—and the AK he was carrying at sling arms—to the soaked ground. It was only then that Ving saw the toe of another boot shooting toward his head.

*Shit! Two of them!*

He ducked his head, and the other boot only struck the side of his skull a glancing blow. Without releasing pressure pinning the arm holding the AK down, Ving swung his heavily muscled left arm out and swept the planted leg of the second man out from under him. Slamming his forearm down on the first man's throat, Ving leapt on the second man, tearing the AK from his arms and then snapping his head sharply to the right. The dull sound of his neck snapping was audible.

Ving heard the sharp hissing ring of a knife blade being drawn from its scabbard and he knew he had screwed up by the numbers. His back muscles tightened and he flinched in anticipation of the feel of cold steel penetrating his flesh. When he didn't feel it, he looked over his shoulder in surprise to see Brad standing over the first man, the smoking suppressor on the end of his Ruger Mark V still aimed at what remained of the soldier's—for that's what he was, a soldier dressed in black fatigues—eye.

"You're gettin' slow in your old age, Ving."

"Awww, I had 'im, Brad, you din't haveta do that."

"You had him all right. He was about to make a shish kabob outta you."

Ving grunted as he rolled the man beneath him over and began to pat him down for anything of intelligence value. He removed a small plastic identity card, a ball point pen, a small notebook containing what looked like chicken scratches on its pages, and a small single foreign coin. Each item he placed in a corresponding pocket on his body. Then he reached for a small two-way radio clipped to the web belt around the soldier's waist.

He glanced up at Brad. "Wanna take these AKs?"

"No, let's just break them down and scatter the parts. I'll carry the bolts back with me and toss them out in the woods on the way back. I'm not sure whether Lamsam would appreciate us giving them to Chakan or not ... probably not."

Ving grunted again as bent over to lift his soldier by the shoulders. "I'll take care of my mess, but I ain't cleanin' up after you, Brad. You shot 'im, you put 'im away."

Brad shoved the Ruger back into its holster and secured the flap. "Come on Ving, I'd think you'd be a little more grateful, me saving your ass and all..." He was smiling. Ving had saved his life more times than he could count. The banter was just their way of dealing with what just happened. Ving was really good at his craft, one of the best Brad had ever seen, and it was incredibly unusual for anyone to get the drop on him. Whoever these dead guys were, they were good.

Brad knelt and patted down the man he had killed. The man looked Chinese, and when Brad glanced at the plastic coated ID he took from a shirt pocket, he recognized the characters as *Hànyǔ Pīnyīn*, the romanization system for standard Chinese on mainland China and in Taiwan. On a hunch, he took out his knife and slit the dead man's sleeve above the elbow and spread it open. He let out a low, soundless whistle as he took in the tattoo he'd been expecting.

"Take a look at this, Ving."

Ving sighed and let his soldier slump to the ground. Turning back, he leaned over the man Brad was searching, his brown eyes narrowing at the sight of the tattoo. He had seen plenty of them on the biceps of Chinese Special Forces troops in Iraq.

"What the hell are Chinese SF types doin' in Thailand?"

"I don't know, Ving, but that sort of explains how these two got the jump on you, doesn't it?"

"They never woulda slipped up on me if it hadn't been for the storm," Ving growled. He was embarrassed. The truth was that he'd been careless. He'd taken it for granted that he was operating on a resort island in Thailand. He'd never expected to encounter competent hostiles here, much less some of the toughest troops in the world.

"What the hell have we gotten ourselves into?" Brad murmured.

* * *

Jared was waiting for them when they returned to the hut, soaked to the bone.

"Thought you guys would have been back before now."

"So did I, but Ving here had to stop and play." Brad's voice dropped its teasing tone. "He got jumped."

Jared turned to Ving. "Oh yeah? How'd that happen?"

"I got careless for a minute, an' they got lucky."

"They?"

"Never expected to see no Chinese Special Forces workin' for no Russian guy ... for Pete's sake, those guys are *enemies*."

"*Zhōnghú Rénmín Jiěfàngjūn tèzhǒng bùduì?*" Jared glanced at Brad for confirmation. "Here?"

Brad nodded. "Both of the ones we took out had the same tattoos on their biceps those guys in Fallujah had ... the unit tattoo."

"Chakan said all the guards on patrol are Chinese," Lamsam broke in, "but I had no idea."

"Not many people know about the *Zhōnghú Rénmín Jiěfàngjūn tèzhǒng bùduì.*" Jared's face told of his concern. "They don't get much press, at least not like our Special Ops people do. The only reason we ever heard of them is because we saw them in action during the second Battle of Fallujah. Nasty tempers, but very well trained … and vicious fighters."

It was Lamsam's turn to be concerned. "This is totally unexpected, I don't know."

"Don't go getting cold feet on us now, inspector. It's too late for us to back out now. Two of our team members are entering that resort right about now, going into harm's way. It's too late to stop them. We won't leave them, no matter what. Period." Brad's eyes were flat, and his voice was cold.

Lamsam's eyes were on Brad's Ruger and on the hand that was perilously close to it. He shrugged. "You have no idea how many of them there are."

"It doesn't matter how many of them are *here*," Brad said evenly. "What we have to worry about is how many Bykov has at the place where he's holding the hostages for ransom."

"Yeah, about that, Brad, there's a new wrinkle in that part of the equation."

"What's that, Jared?"

"The chopper doesn't fly in to pick them up. There's a man-made underground hangar inside the resort. The chopper is parked inside."

"Shit! We're going to have to mount a round-the-clock watch on that hangar."

"Yeah, I was thinkin' the same thing. He could take them outta there at any time. The good news is that there's a big ol' banyan tree outside the perimeter that gives a perfect view of the hangar door. The door is camouflaged pretty good ... the only reason I saw it was because they had it open for some reason. When they close it, it's hard to spot, even when you just saw it open."

Brad frowned. "We need to get started right away. I've got a feeling things are going to speed up when those two guys don't show up for their reliefs."

## Chapter Eighteen

**Pleasures, second day of Vicky and Jessica's stay.**

Vicky languished indolently on the king-sized bed, wearing nothing more than the flimsiest transparent beach cover-up that covered everything and concealed nothing. She was careful to remain in front of the concealed pin cameras as much as possible when she was in the suite, and every time she went out, she delighted in changing into her various ensembles.

*He's a man and not a bad-looking one at that ... and the care he takes with his dress and his grooming ... wow! I can tell by the way he moves that he is very fit regardless of his age. And those hands!*

She shivered visibly beneath the sheer fabric. Vicky turned so the cameras would catch her in profile, knowing somehow that he was watching her. She was also extremely conscious of Fly's drone silently moving around the room, watching her every move. The knowledge that both Bykov and Brad were watching her was exhilarating. She had always loved teasing men, but she had never done it to two men at the same time. Nor had she ever been as brazen as she had been since she had reached Pleasures. The tingling in her lower belly radiated out in all directions, causing her to quiver repeatedly.

*I have been looking forward to this ever since we came up with this plan, but I had absolutely no idea that actually doing it would turn me on so much!*

\* \* \*

Brad had watched Vicky's arrival at Pleasures on his pocket monitor through the micro drone's miniature eye. Vicky's performance before the cameras had incited conflicting emotions in him as he watched it. It had aroused him tremendously, but he had also experienced intense jealousy. He and Vicky had not made a firm lifetime commitment to monogamy, but it still rankled to know that another man was watching Vicky's frankly erotic display. This was the woman who shared his bed, but he was surprised at his proprietary attitude toward her. The lecherous looks she'd received from other men had always amused him before, but now he found himself disturbed by the idea.

*Maybe this wasn't such a good idea ... might be better if Fly set an alarm on her drone that would let us know when she's moving. One on Jess's too, I don't think I could handle watching that. I really should have thought this through. I need to get on the horn with Fly ASAP and see what she can do about that.*

* * *

"Well looky here." Vicky was standing in the doorway joining her suite with Jessica's, leaning against the jamb and waving an elegant white card, an engraved invitation to dinner from Bykov.

Jessica smiled knowingly and waved her own invitation back in response.

"I guess we'd better get ready then, hadn't we?" Vicky turned and went into her suite to get dressed. Her heart was pounding and she had to work to keep her breathing in check. She forced herself to slow down, keeping her movements smooth and expressive, allowing herself to show her pleasure at the invitation. Careful to stay within range of the pin cameras, she undressed like a woman anticipating a sexual encounter and then ran a tub full of water. She chose exotically scented oils from the generous selection provided and added them to the water before settling in the tub.

*Watch me you bastard! You'll get closer before this is over, I have no doubt, and I'm not completely sure I'm going to hate that. I promise you one thing though: I'll see you led away in cuffs at the end of this op, and that's a promise!*

When she dried off and dressed, she heard the tiniest buzz as Fly's drone settled in one of the folds of the sea-green gown she was wearing. Cut daringly low, nearly to her navel, and slit high on her hip, the gown was a male fantasy come true. She wore nothing beneath it, and the décolletage exposed the soft curve of her breasts almost to her areolae. If she took too deep a breath, she would be exposed. She felt her nipples harden at the thought. She was ready.

\* \* \*

*Too soon! Too soon! It is not like him to rush a selection like this. We should have waited at least another week. It doesn't matter, he's the boss, and I'll do as he says even if I believe he's wrong. Bykov is fond of having his orders obeyed, and I have seen firsthand what happens to subordinates who disobey him, even me.*

*Everything is ready. The chopper crew is prepared to roll the bird out of the hangar as soon as I text them. I've got drinks ready for the ladies and I have the packets of Rohypnol in my cuffs. The chef has the meal ready and the servants are standing by. They will eat well tonight, that's for sure. Why Bykov wants to change the protocol and give them the drugs in the aperitif is beyond me. He must be really hot for that redhead. Not that I blame him, she's gorgeous and she's obviously looking for a little action, that's been evident since the moment she got here. If the boss wasn't so enamored of her I'd have given that a shot myself! I just hope this change in the protocol doesn't screw anything up. Okay Mikhail, here goes nothing!*

\* \* \*

Charlie leaned uncomfortably back on a thick limb in the banyan tree. He glanced down at his wrist chronograph and noted that there were only eighteen minutes left before Jared was due to relieve him. All of them had taken turns in the tree, and the leaves and branches had been judiciously pruned away, leaving a clear view of the camouflaged hangar door where the H-225 was concealed, but nothing had been done to make the damned thing more comfortable. Even Ving's bulk hadn't softened the perch up any.

Charlie stretched cautiously, moving his arms and legs to get his blood flowing in preparation for the climb down. He was startled mid-stretch by the sound of the concealed hangar door as it began to rise slowly. Leaning forward, bracing his hands against a tree limb, he watched as a black-clad Chinese on an electric tow tractor dragged the H-225 out onto the helipad. He was followed by two men in flight suits, who immediately began a preflight inspection.

"They just got the bird out, Brad, something's happening," he whispered. The earwig Fly had gotten for all Team Dallas members was a technological marvel, and it picked up the whisper and transmitted it instantaneously into every member of the team, even Fly back in Texas.

Brad's response was immediate. "Fly! You got movement on Vicky and Jess?"

"Slowing heart rate on both, Brad, just started. No movement yet."

Unable to wait to ask, Brad flicked on the drone-cam monitor and couldn't get a picture to form. Vicky's drone was dormant, apparently hidden in a fold of her dress.

"Got movement now, Brad!"

Charlie observed four gurneys being wheeled out toward the large chopper. Bykov's men hadn't even bothered to cover them or even strap them down. "They're taking them out to the chopper! We've gotta stop them!" He began to slither down the trunk of the banyan, cursing inwardly because he only had the suppressed Ruger Mark V with him.

"No, Charlie—stand fast!" Brad hated to give the order, his heart was pounding and his primal instinct was to keep the chopper from lifting off with his cousin and his lover. Only the iron will of his warrior side kept him from trying to stop it. "We've come too far, Charlie; we've got to see this through. Stick there until the chopper lifts off and then get back here as quickly as possible without letting them see you." He hesitated for a second before speaking again. "They look okay, don't they? Don't appear to be hurt?"

"Not as far as I can see," Charlie muttered, furious and worried at the same time.

"Ving!"

"Already movin' Brad!" Ving and Jared had already taken the RB-15 over to Jomtien Beach and slipped inside the warehouse. They had been sitting in battered old steel chairs in the warehouse, sipping bad instant coffee and waiting for the action to start. As soon as Charlie had alerted Brad, Ving had raced to the Isuzu Bison and fired it up while Jared opened the warehouse door. Ving stopped the truck just past the door and waited impatiently as Jared secured it behind them.

"Pete!"

"On it, Brad! Doing my preflight now, already got the radar up and going."

Brad turned to Lamsam, who was hunched over a primitive table made of split bamboo and looking apprehensive as hell. "Get ready, inspector. As soon as Charlie gets back we're headed for the mouth of the creek."

"I don't know, Brad, maybe I should let somebody know…"

"No way in hell, inspector," Brad said, his face frozen in deadly earnest. "I can't let you do that."

"Brad, we are breaking my country's laws, laws I have sworn to uphold."

"And you are talking about putting my team—*my family*—at risk. That's not going to happen. In an hour, hopefully less, we will be in the air and technically no longer in your country. If you can't live with that, then I will leave you here."

Lamsam sighed heavily and got to his feet. "I'm sorry, I cannot allow this." His hand went to the service weapon on his hip.

"Yes you can," Charlie muttered from the open doorway, his voice cold as death. In his hands he held the Ruger, and the suppressor was aimed unwaveringly at Lamsam's left eye.

Brad's smile was a grim one. "Your choice, inspector. You're either in or out. We have no time for indecisiveness right now and no room for it on this mission."

Lamsam's head never moved, his eyes alone shifting from Charlie to Brad and back to Charlie again.

*These men aren't playing. I can either go along with this or I will never see my family again. Why did I ever agree to this?*

Lamsam heaved a huge sigh. "I am in. I hope you know this could mean the end of my career."

"Sorry about that, inspector, but the lives of two people very special to me depend on me having the freedom to do whatever is necessary, and, believe me, I will … no matter what it takes." He didn't have to say, "Even if I have to kill you;" the look on Lamsam's face told him the man got the message loud and clear.

Charlie advanced on Lamsam with the intention of relieving the inspector of his sidearm, but Brad held up a staying hand.

"I don't think that will be necessary, Charlie … will it, inspector?"

Lamsam locked eyes with Brad. *I may either accept this or he is going to stop me from being able to notify my superiors. I made a decision before and now I regret it. The only hope I have of salvaging this now is to go along with him and try to limit the damage. On the bright side, if he succeeds, I will become chief of Special Branch. It is a gamble, but it is all I have left.*

"No. It will not be necessary. I give you my word." He meant it.

"Good. Let's get to the cliff. Ving and Jared should be there in an hour or so, and I want to get in the air as soon as possible after they get here." Brad deliberately turned his back on Lamsam and waved to Charlie. "Grab your gear, we need to make tracks."

* * *

The RB-15 came in fast, Ving reversing the thrust of the outboard at the last possible second before nosing it onto the rocks. Brad, Charlie, and Lamsam tossed their backpacks into the boat and leaped inside even as the rubber nose of the craft bounced off the rocks and rebounded out into deeper water.

"Jared, you out in the bird?" Pete had taxied the Martin PBM-5 in closer to shore after Ving and Jared loaded the weapons and ordnance aboard it. Brad could see the big aircraft floating in the bay, its engines idling slowly.

"Yeah Brad, Pete has this bird up and running an' I'm standing in this doorway, winch cable in my hand!"

"And I'm tracking the drones on the chopper."

"Thanks Fly." Brad marveled yet again at the clarity and the real-time response of the tiny earwigs she had given them. "Where are they headed?"

"Can't be certain, Brad. I expected them to head for Bangkok, but it looks as if the chopper is headed out across the bay on a northwesterly heading. That chopper has a lot of range, but I'll be damned if I can see any place significant along that path."

Brad felt his gut churn. *Where the hell are they going?*

# Chapter Nineteen

### Bay of Bangkok, present day.

"Sneaky bastards! They just dropped below radar coverage, Brad, but they don't know about the drones!"

"Where are they now, Fly?" Brad was staring at the radar screen in the cockpit of the Martin, where the blip representing Bykov's helicopter had just vanished without a trace.

"The only thing I can see up there is an old monastery. The satellite images are showing a helluva heat signature there. No way human bodies could give off that much heat in such an old stone building, the stone would mask that. It's just an educated guess, Brad, but I'd say that ancient edifice has been modernized—electricity and a heating and cooling system. That chopper appears to be headed straight for it."

"Get me some aerials of the place ASAP, Fly." Brad turned to Pete. "Find a place to set this bird down, Pete, now!"

"On it, Brad. Looks like a lake big enough to handle us, about ten miles from where we are right now."

"No place we can set her on the ground?" The Martin could land on hard ground, but the suspension wouldn't handle a rough strip, it had to be improved.

"No way. That lake, Khao Laem Lake, is in some kind of national park, but there's not a flat piece of terrain between here and there."

"Do it!"

"Wish we coulda brought the Mrazors man," Ving drawled. "My dogs are gonna be barkin' big time by the time we get to that monastery."

"I wish we woulda brought some chutes; that woulda made it easier." Jared was chuckling. He knew very well that Ving was an expert parachutist, but the man hated doing it and avoided it like the plague when there was another option available.

"Hey, it's ten miles from where we are right now, but it's only about a mile and a half from the monastery. It's steep terrain, and from what I can tell it's rugged, but it ain't that far to walk."

"I'm more concerned about pursuit after we get the women out," Brad muttered. "What about the approaches, Fly?"

"All wooded as far as I can tell, Brad. The only road comes in from the east, and it just looks like a well-used dirt track. Sending out aerials to your monitors now. The bad news is the route from that lake to the monastery is pretty rough terrain, you're going to be traveling up a pretty steep incline through heavily forested mountain terrain."

Ving, Jared, and Charlie were already making adjustments to the five rucksacks, splitting up the ordnance as evenly as possible. The ammo and drum magazines for the AA-12s were already broken down into chest packs. The chest packs for Brad and Ving were heavier because of the spare drums for the American 180s.

"Mule train," Ving muttered. "The Corps thought I was some kinda pack mule too."

Brad smiled to himself. He had seen Ving carry loads that would have been impossible for a lesser man to carry for many miles over torturous terrain and then fight for days without rest or sleep. The man was made of iron.

"I know you've got your hands full, Fly, but I need you to see if you can deploy the drones inside the monastery and get me some idea of the layout and the forces inside as soon as you can."

"I'm on it, Brad. I've got Vicky's drone airborne already. They put Vicky and Jessica both inside rooms somewhere inside. They seem to be unconscious, but their vitals are all in the green. I'm working on Jessica's drone now, but I'm having some trouble finding a way out into the corridor with it. I can feed you intel while you're walking up there. This place is huge."

\* \* \*

There was no way to conceal the giant aircraft with its 118 foot wingspan, so Pete disabled the Martin by the simple expedient of pulling the magnetos for the engines and hiding them in a secret compartment in the rear of the fuselage. He anchored the flying boat while Brad and the others launched the RB-15. The last one out, Pete locked the modified cargo doors while standing in the rubber boat. Without knowing the size and strength of the opposition forces in the monastery, Team Dallas could not afford to leave him behind with the aircraft. One man armed with an AA-12 was a significant addition to their firepower.

The forest was trackless, and Fly had been right, the incline was steep and the terrain rugged. Only the superb conditioning the Corps had taught them to maintain and sheer willpower enabled the team to keep moving toward their objective. None of them wasted any breath talking as they climbed; rather, they listened carefully to the steady patter of information Fly was relaying over their earwigs. Each of them was building a mental image of the inside of the monastery through her words. Fly was recording physical images that she could edit and then transmit when they stopped infrequently to orient themselves and when Brad finally designated their objective rally point.

The going was slow, much slower than they were used to traveling, even on foot. Shortly into their climb, all five men heard Fly's sharp intake of breath over their earwigs.

"Brad, I don't like the looks of this—there is a corridor running parallel to the one where Vicky and Jessica are being held. It's set up like a barracks; I think these used to be monks' cells…"

"How many, Fly?"

"I count twenty to a side, but I can't tell you how many of them are occupied. The doors are closed and there is no noise at all in here."

Brad glanced down at his wristwatch, noting that the time was zero two thirty-three hours.

"That ain't good, brother," Ving said. "Them guys are used ta bein' packed together like sardines in a can. Monks' cells or not, they could be bunkin' four at a time in there—could be a couple hundred guys stashed away in that corridor."

"Yeah," Charlie interjected, "and Fly hasn't covered the whole place yet. We could be looking at a lot more if there's another corridor. That's one helluva big monastery."

"You may need to rethink this, Brad. Charlie's right; I haven't covered all of this place yet, not by a long shot. There's no telling how many people Bykov has inside, and that's just too many guns."

"There's no way we're leaving Vicky and Jess inside there, Fly. This always was a risky op—I knew that from the start." Something Jess had said to him back at the ranch came back to him. "Jess said something about these monasteries when we were planning the op order. She said that not all of the orders of monks were warriors and that some of them were persecuted. She said most of these stone structures had secret entrances and exits. Find me a way in, Fly. I never really thought we could storm the front gates anyway."

"Roger that, Brad!" Fly's voice was filled with grim determination.

"We need to give that girl a raise," Ving remarked. "Whatever we're paying her ain't enough." Despite the rigors of the climb he was not even breathing heavily.

"We're just a little way from the summit, Fly. We'll be setting up the objective rally point shortly thereafter. I need some footage of the east side of that monastery, up close and personal."

"I can deploy one of the drones outside, Brad, but we are going to run the risk of losing it. I've only got another hour and a half charge on the battery, and it's going to use a lot more power fighting the winds outside." She was already moving Vicky's drone toward the sole entrance. She knew Brad didn't give a damn about losing the drone, not with Vicky's and Jessica's lives hanging in the balance.

* * *

Once they crossed over the military crest of the far side of the steep hill, they could see the outlines of the monastery through the trees. Brad raised his fist in the signal to halt and then rotated his fist, index finger raised, in a circular motion to indicate that he was designating the spot they were in as their objective rallying point. Without hesitation all four team members spread out in a 360° defensive perimeter, their bodies prone, weapons pointed outward. Inspector Lamsam lay down between Ving and Jared, but instead of looking outward he rolled onto his side and watched Brad. He had heard only one side of the conversations between Brad and Fly, but what he'd heard had disturbed him. Brad settled in the center of the perimeter.

"Send me the feed, Fly, and talk to me."

"Hold on a second, Brad," Fly responded testily. "I've got my hands full flying two drones simultaneously in two places and I've been sending you video that's already stored in your monitor's memory. I think I've found something here—a section of the wall on the east side of the monastery that appears to be made out of a different type of stone than the rest of the wall. I never would've spotted it if I hadn't followed a declivity running down to the back wall from a spot about a hundred meters to your right." She had spotted the declivity quite by accident. From ground level she would never have noticed it, but from the vantage point of the drone at treetop level, the ruler-straight depression in the foliage of the treetops was clearly visible.

When she had rotated the drone and focused on the back wall of the monastery, she had not noticed the difference in coloration of the stones at first, but when she had switched camera capability to infrared, the variation had stood out like a sore thumb. The thermal signature of the different stone in the wall clearly delineated a man-height arched shape.

"This has got to be the entrance to a tunnel, Brad. It's the right shape and height, but I'll be damned if I can figure out how to open it. You're going to have to go hands-on. I'm sending the infrared images to your monitor now."

"Thanks Fly. Keep doing your magic. I need you to keep looking for personnel with one of the drones, but I need you to get one of them back to keep an eye on Vicky and Jessica."

"Roger that," Fly said with an exasperated sigh. *Damn right it's magic!*

\* \* \*

Brad summoned all four team members and Lamsam into the center of the ORP, violating the team's SOP (standard operating procedure). The situation he was faced with did not conform to any contingency that had ever occurred to him, and frankly neither did the rest of the crazy mission. *It's my own damned fault. I never should have let*

*Vicky and Jess talk me into this, I knew better. I didn't have adequate intel to plan a mission like this! Dammit, I knew better, and now I've not only put Vicky and Jess at risk, I'm about to put my four closest friends in jeopardy in a situation I'm not sure I can get them out of safely. What a miserable mess!*

He looked each man dead in the eye in turn before he spoke. "You all heard what Fly said, except for you, inspector." He proceeded to give Lamsam a brief but concise rundown of the facts as Fly had related them to him.

"We are grossly outnumbered. I only see one option available to us to continue this mission, and I hate like hell to ask you to do it..."

"Save it, Brad," Ving muttered. "No way in hell we're leaving Vicky and Jess inside that place, so drop the apologies. We all knew there was a risk when we agreed to this mission without enough information for an adequate end plan. We been through enough shit together to know that sometimes a good plan falls to pieces anyway, so go ahead and tell us what you're thinking."

"I'm in, Brad," Jared said somberly.

"So am I—you knew you didn't even have to ask me." Charlie's face was a mask of determination. Pete didn't have to say a word, he just nodded his head. Brad felt a surge of pride as he surveyed the members of his team. The emotion he felt choked him up, and it was a moment before he could speak. He cleared his throat.

"That leaves you, inspector. I'll understand if you decide to go back and wait by the aircraft until we return, but you'll understand that we can't take a chance on you contacting your superiors before we can get Vicky and Jess out of the monastery. Pete will tell you how to get back aboard the aircraft, and you'll be able to use the radio inside. By the time you make it back to the lake we'll either be on our way back or…"

Lamsam didn't hesitate. *This is insane, but I have no choice. If they don't succeed at this point my career is over and I will be shamed before my father and grandfather. What is that quaint American saying, 'In for a penny; in for a pound'?* He stared pointedly down at his sidearm and then up at the AA-12 in Brad's hands. Brad took the hint, and without hesitation handed over the shotgun. After a moment's hesitation, he removed his chest pack and lifted out the drum magazines for the American 180 and placed them in a waterproof bag from his rucksack. In seconds he fashioned a strap out of para cord and slung the waterproof bag across his chest. Unslinging the American 180, he inserted a drum magazine and tapped it into place.

"There's no other explanation for the anomaly Fly located on the east wall of the monastery. It has to be one of those secret entrances Jess had talked about."

"Yeah, now all we have to do is figure out how to get inside. We may have to use a shape charge to get that tunnel open, and that's going to really screw with the element of surprise—which is the only thing we really have going for us."

"Not necessarily, Jared. We can scrape at the mortar and see just how deep that wall really is. Maybe that's just a thin cover, maybe we can use det cord."

Lamsam spoke up. "I may be able to help you there. There are many such monasteries in Thailand, and I am familiar with the most commonly used mechanisms to secure the doors. Most of them are not really secret entrances, at least that was not their original purpose. Some orders of monks, particularly the militant ones, were persecuted by the monarchy or local warlords. In the event of a siege, it was convenient for the monks to have an escape route. I am somewhat surprised that there should be one so obvious on the back wall. I would have expected a subterranean escape tunnel that would be more difficult to spot."

"There's nothing else we can do from here that's going to do us a bit of good," Charlie said softly. "According to what Jess has told me, some of these escape tunnels just have a thin façade concealing them. If they used this one for a secret entrance as well as an exit, they would not have wanted to hang around outside for very long if there was a chance someone might be watching them."

Brad stood up, dusting off the legs of his trousers with his hands. Then he glanced down at his wristwatch once more. 0307 hours. "There's not much time left before daylight."

Ving stood up easily, as if he was not burdened with a rucksack and a chest pack that, combined, weighed as much as a normal man. He slung his American 180 over his shoulder and lifted his AA-12 to the port arms position after tapping in his magazine and jacking a round into the chamber. "Yeah, it's time to beat feet."

Jared took point, and the others followed in single file, ten meters apart. They were moving fast.

# Chapter Twenty

**Logovo, 0346 hours.**

They were all flattened against the stone wall in the shadows except for Jared and Inspector Lamsam. Jared had scraped and probed at the mortar between the stones and discovered that the slightly off-colored stones were merely a veneer covering some sort of frame. He and the inspector were frantically searching for the trip mechanism for the door.

"I have it," Lamsam hissed. There was a distinct click and a solid gap materialized in the wall, outlining the hidden door. Lamsam dug his fingers into the crack and pulled, feeling the tips of his fingernails bending backwards as he did so. There was an awful creaking sound as the door resisted his efforts, but as soon as Jared could get his fingers in the gap, he inserted them and began to tug as well.

As soon as the door was open sufficiently for Ving's broad shoulders to pass through, he slipped on his night vision goggles and entered the Stygian darkness of the tunnel. Through the eyes of the night vision device the stone walls appeared a ghastly green. A slightly phosphorescent moss covered the damp stone giving the tunnel an eerie kind of glow. Ving's broad nostrils flared as he sniffed the air. There was a musty smell, but he was having no trouble breathing. He decided to test the earwig's transmission capability inside the tunnel.

"Looks clear to me, Brad," he whispered. "Fly, you copy?"

"Not quite as clearly as before, Ving, but I'm reading you 3x5 ... maybe 4x5. I'm going to switch over and use the drones as retransmitters when I start losing the signal. All that stone is impeding the signals."

Jared was next to enter the tunnel, his AA-12 at the ready. Night vision goggles in place, he moved gingerly down the tunnel, his sharp eyes searching for booby traps and other devices designed to impede the progress of intruders. He was followed closely by the inspector, who peered over his shoulder at the tunnel ahead, his hand on Jared's shoulder. Ving instinctively dropped back and let Jared take the lead. They were followed in turn by Brad, Charlie, and Pete, who pulled the door shut behind them.

Brad trusted Jared implicitly, and he made no effort to urge the man forward or to hasten the pace despite a growing sense of urgency in his gut. Something simply did not feel right.

* * *

Vicky awakened slowly, recognizing the residual effects of the Rohypnol for what they were. She forced herself to remain still, her eyes closed, as she returned to full awareness, concentrating on the sounds and smells around her. The skimpy designer dress she had worn to dinner with Bykov was in disarray, and her breasts were exposed. A fleeting memory of Bykov caressing her at the dinner table flashed through her mind unbidden. His hands had been exactly what she'd expected—strong, experienced, and profoundly erotic. He had instinctively known what it would take to arouse her, and she had been responding in spite of herself when the Rohypnol took effect and she slipped from consciousness. Only her extensive training in resisting the effect of drugs had enabled her to retain her memory of the last few minutes before she passed out.

Forcing the memory from her mind, Vicky concentrated on the sounds and the *feel* of the room she was in. She sensed that the room was not large, perhaps half the size of a small bedroom. There was an unmistakable odor of dank stone permeating the air, despite the sound of the air handler from a large central heat and air conditioning system. When the air handler stopped pushing air, she listened for sounds of life on the other side of the door to her room. Nothing.

Vicky allowed her eyelids to raise slightly so that she could get her first visual impression. She didn't dare move her head, suspecting, rightly, that there would be pin cameras in the room recording her every move. The room, what she could see of it, was appointed sparsely although pleasantly, with clean, modern furnishings.

Pretending that she was just coming to, Vicky sat up on the edge of the bed. She stretched awkwardly and clumsily, allowing her fingers to run lightly over the folds in her dress. Fly's drone was missing. *Crap! Did they find it or is it out scouting around? Surely Fly would have deployed the drone instead of letting it fall into Bykov's hands...*

She stood up hesitantly, staggering as if she were still under the effects of the drug, and walked over to the single door in the room. Locked. There was a single peephole in the door, and Vicky leaned forward, pressing her eye close in order to get as much of a look outside as she could. What she saw was a long hallway with other doors evenly spaced on both sides.

*All I can do now is wait. Either wait for Bykov to make his next move or wait for Brad and the guys to come for me. I wish we'd had better intel, but we had to go with what we had. I have to believe that Jess is in one of these other rooms in the hallway, and no doubt those other women are here too. As interesting as it might be to find out whether Bykov lives up to his advance billing as a lover, I'm a little nervous about what happens next. Brad—where are you?*

\* \* \*

Lamsam's expertise proved invaluable in the tunnel. Three times he halted Jared by the simple expedient of clamping down on his shoulder. Each time he pointed out a primitive but effective device designed to injure or kill intruders. Each time, he managed to trip the device without injury to any of the team.

"I hope they ain't no alarm hooked up to that thing," Ving muttered under his breath.

Lamsam looked over his shoulder at the massive black man, a green shadow seen through the eyepiece of his night vision device. "I don't believe there is. These devices are ancient, probably as old as the monastery itself."

"Makes me nervous anyway. We need to git out of this tunnel ASAP! The quicker we git this done the quicker I kin git home—the bacon in Bangkok leaves a little somethin' to be desired."

Ving grumbling when they were tactical was an unusual occurrence, and Brad picked up on it. "Move out, Jared," he whispered. His gut sense of impending disaster was growing by the moment.

The end of the tunnel came as a surprise to them, appearing just past the apex of a hard turn to the left. The exit door had a simple doorknob that required only a twist to open. All of them, knowing that visible light seen through the night vision devices would blind them, had slipped off the devices and blinked their eyes rapidly several times before Jared whispered that he was about to open the door.

The instant the door was open Jared sprang into the hallway, followed closely by Ving, who nearly knocked Lamsam off his feet brushing past him. The two men faced opposite directions in the hallway, their weapons leveled and ready for combat. There was no one in the hallway.

"It's about time you guys found your way in here! I was beginning to worry." Fly's voice, retransmitted through the drone to their earwigs, was as clear as if she were standing right next to them. All of them except Lamsam, who had no earwig, blinked in amazement at the effectiveness of the incredible technology Fly had given the team.

Brad was grateful but not distracted. "Where are they, Fly?"

"Six doors down on the left, in the direction Jared is facing. You caught a break, Brad. Your emergency tunnel opened up on the corridor where Bykov keeps his hostages. Vicky is in the room on the left and Jessica is across the hall. The infrared cameras indicate that there are five more women on the corridor." Brad had already shoved past Jared and was hurrying down toward Vicky's door. "I will tell you which of the rooms hold hostages as you get to them."

"We can look through the peepholes, Fly; tell us where the hostiles are!" Brad was counting down the doors on the left. Ving stayed where he was, covering the rear, while the others checked the peepholes quickly and methodically.

*Track Down Thailand*

\* \* \*

"Why don't you get yourself a cup of coffee, Pavel? You look like you've been awake for three days."

Pavel Stravinsky rubbed his bleary eyes with his fists and stood up from his chair at the security console. "Thank you, comrade! I'm pulling a double shift; Kaparov has a stomach virus and I volunteered to replace him. My eyes feel like they have sand in them."

Orel nodded his understanding but made a mental note to take disciplinary action against Kaparov. He had little sympathy for shirkers, and this was not the first time Kaparov had missed his shift over some minor or imagined ailment. The few Russian nationals at Logovo were paid lavishly, and there was no excuse for goofing off.

Stravinsky stumbled off to the break area to grab a cup of the strong black Russian tea he preferred to coffee and to quickly smoke one of his precious

*Belomorkanal* cigarettes. The brand was produced in the Ukraine and had a reputation as one of the strongest cigarettes in Eastern Europe, if not the strongest in the world. Orel was fanatical about not permitting smoking in the communications room, and it had been several hours since Stravinsky had been able to take his last break.

Orel sat down at the console and reached for the small bottle of hand sanitizer that he kept in one of the cubbyholes of the desk and wiped his hands down. Then he removed one of the sterile wipes from its container, wiping down the keyboard and mouse. After he had gone through his cleaning ritual, he unlocked one of the desk drawers and removed his personal wireless headset.

He began to scan through the monitors in each of the cells in which the women were kept as was his custom. The very first cell he checked was Vicky's as he was intensely attracted to the sexy redhead. *There is something about that woman that drives me absolutely wild. Too bad Bykov has the hots for her too. I would've liked to tap that one myself, but no way am I going to cross the old man. The hottest woman in the world would not be worth doing that, he's too damned vengeful.*

Vicky was just beginning to stretch and Orel's eyes were riveted on her perfect breasts. He watched her longer than he had intended and then reluctantly switched to a new camera. The blonde woman that had come in with the redhead seemed to have overcome the effects of the Rohypnol a little faster than the redhead. She seemed to be more alert and was moving around more easily.

Orel began to check the other women's cells, though more peremptorily. The last woman he checked was standing at her cell door, trying to peer through the peephole. As he watched, he saw her began to pound on the door with her fists, and he could see her mouth moving. Quickly, he turned up the volume.

"Help! I'm in here! Help!" She was pounding furiously on the door.

Panic flooded Orel's body and he instantly switched to the corridor camera. There were six heavily armed men in the corridor, and all but two of the women had already been released from their cells. He didn't bother turning up the volume. Using his fist, he slammed the red button on the console and a monstrously loud klaxon horn began to sound throughout the monastery.

* * *

Brad had barely finished handing over the earwigs to Vicky and Jessica when the alarm began to sound. The noise was so loud that he could literally feel it in his chest. "Shit!" He grabbed Vicky's wrist and turned to go back the same way he had come in, but at that moment the door at the end of the corridor slammed open and black-clad Asians began to pour through it.

Ving dropped into a combat crouch instinctively and unleashed the awesome firepower of the American 180. The high-pitched ripping sound was audible even over the racket from the klaxon horns. As he emptied the first drum magazine down the narrow corridor, the black-clad Chinese fell to the floor like a child's jackstraws. He calmly but quickly cast the empty drum magazine to the floor and pulled another from his chest pack in a smooth, practiced motion and tapped it into place.

"The other way, Brad! The other way!"

There wasn't room for two shooters to stand side by side in the corridor, and Brad quickly turned, shouting into his earwig. "Go, go, go!" He gave Vicky a rough shove, and the team and women began to race toward the far end of the corridor, with Jessica in the lead.

"Last door on the left, Jess!" Fly's voice was calm and emotionless. "It opens onto a wider corridor. I'm not sure what it's for, supplies maybe, but it doesn't appear to have any cells along the sides and it's headed toward the back wall. I've got your drone moving along it right now!"

Cursing under his breath, Brad urged the women to follow Jess while constantly checking over his shoulder. "Ving! Come on!"

He needn't have bothered. Ving was rapidly backpedaling down the corridor, calmly unloading drum magazines into the Chinese troops, who seemed to keep coming through the door despite the bodies of their comrades littering the floor.

"Crazy bastards jist keep comin', Brad! Y'all get the hell out of the way, I'm comin' through!" Looking back over his shoulder, Ving saw Brad standing in a doorway on the left side of the corridor and staring toward him anxiously. Inserting one more drum magazine into the American 180, he turned and fled, ignoring the first shots fired by the lead Chinese soldier. He felt the sting of a round as it penetrated his trousers and grazed his right calf.

"Get the hell out of the way, Brad, go, go, go!" As he ducked inside the doorway, Ving removed the American 180 from his shoulder and slung the AA-12 in its place. He jacked one of the large magazines into the 12-gauge and took up a position in the doorway.

Jared pulled away from the group of women and went back to Ving and Brad. "Go on, Brad, I got this." Brad did not hesitate. The hostages were his responsibility, and there was no one on Earth he trusted more to have his back than Ving and Jared. He ran toward the women just as he heard the booming percussion from Ving's AA-12 as the big man sent a hellish hailstorm of double-aught buckshot into the advancing Chinese. Despite the deadly rain of lead pellets, each roughly the size of a twenty-two caliber round, the Chinese kept coming.

"Some a them guys must be wearin' body armor!"

"If they ain't, they's one hell of a lot more of 'em than Fly let on!"

"I only had time to check two of those corridors, Ving. There's no way I could've given you a more accurate count, you guys moved faster than I expected you to." Tension was beginning to creep into Fly's voice. People under less stress than Team Dallas was at the moment might have detected a trace of resentment as well.

Looking back over his shoulder at Ving and Jared, Brad suddenly encountered Pete's substantial body, halted in the wider corridor. "What the hell?" Charlie, Pete, and Vicky were jammed up against the hostages, and Jess and the inspector were bent over at the waist examining something on the wall to Brad's right. "What the hell, Jess?"

"There's a doorway here, Brad! It leads outside, I can smell the dank air coming through the cracks!"

"So go ahead! Bykov has an army chasing us down this damned corridor!"

"We can't find a handle or a lock! There's an inscription here, but I'm not sure what it says, it's in Khmer ... Cambodian, but I've seen it before, I know it."

Brad jerked his head around and stared back at Jared and Ving. "Charlie, Pete, go back and cover Ving and Jared. Ving!"

"I'm kinda busy at the moment, Brad."

"I'm sending Charlie and Pete back up to you. Fallujah!"

Ving and Jared both understood the reference instantly. During the second battle of Fallujah in December of 2004, they had conducted what the brass euphemistically referred to as a 'retrograde' action. Ving had called it what it was, a withdrawal by fire. The technique they had employed was a kind of leapfrog exercise, with elements on either side of the street providing covering fire while the lead elements retreated for ten or twenty meters and halted to provide covering fire for the new lead element to move behind them in turn. The idea was to keep retreating until they were able to break contact.

*   *   *

Jess stared at the inscription on the door. "និយាយមិត្តហើយចូល." She struggled to pronounce the words phonetically, but it was inspector Lamsam who said them. "*Niyeay mitt haey chaul.*"

"Speak friend, and enter," she muttered. "I remember! But what am I supposed to say?"

Lamsam thought for a moment. "I hesitate to correct your translation…"

"Jesus, inspector, correct me, correct me!"

Lamsam did not even look up. "A more accurate translation would be, 'Say friend and enter.'"

"Friend," Jessica screamed. Nothing happened.

Lamsam stepped in front of her, putting his mouth close to the wall. "*Mitt phokte!*" With a loud screech, the door began to open but with agonizing slowness.

Brad stared over the gaggle of wailing females at the door inching open and then back over his shoulder. Bykov's troops were pouring through the door at the end of the corridor despite the deadly barrage being laid down by Ving and Jared. Charlie was limping and Pete looked as if he might have taken a hit. As Brad was watching he was shoving the woman in front of him forward with his left hand, urging her into the narrow opening in the wall. Over the deafening roar of gunfire, he heard Jared scream.

"Go! Run for it!" Jared was reaching into his chest pack as he was yelling, and Brad's eyes widened as he saw Jared's big hand come out with two baseball-sized fragmentation grenades.

"Run," he roared, raising his right fist and making a pumping motion with it, the standard signal to hurry up.

Jared never looked back to see if Ving, Charlie, and Pete were well away. With his left hand he pulled the pins on both grenades, his broad right hand closed around the spoons to keep them from springing off and arming the grenades. With a wind up that would have done credit to a major league baseball pitcher, he threw the two grenades into the gaggle of oncoming Chinese and turned to run, bent over in a crouch.

Even though Jared moved quickly, the massive concussion from the two fragmentation grenades knocked him off his feet. When Brad had seen him throw, he had screamed at the three retreating team members to get down, setting the example by doing a face plant of his own onto the concrete floor. The concussion from the double blast made his ears hurt, and he actually felt the earwig move deeper into his ear canal.

Ears still ringing, he struggled onto all fours and moved toward Charlie, the closest to him. Charlie was sprawled out on the concrete floor, unmoving. Behind him, Pete had his hands over his ears, and Ving was low crawling back toward Jared, who was still lying face down on the floor. The corridor behind Jared was littered with black-clad body parts, and the pristine white walls had turned a dull, mottled red and black. Brad breathed a sigh of relief as he saw Ving helping Jared to his feet. He tried to speak, but he could not hear his own voice. Again he raised his right fist, making the pumping motion. Everything seemed to be moving in slow motion, as if the five of them were walking across the bottom of a swimming pool filled with Jell-O.

Brad ushered them urgently into the opening left by the hidden door just as another wave of Bykov's Chinese flooded the corridor, slipping and stumbling over the bloody remains of their comrades, all the while firing their weapons. Panting heavily, Brad stepped inside the tunnel and turned to tug the concealed door shut. He felt Ving reach over his shoulder and add his muscles to the effort. The stubborn door finally yielded and it shut with a slam. He did not have to tell the others to haul ass. Disoriented as they all were, their instincts had them racing to catch up with the others.

# Chapter Twenty-one

**Leaving Logovo**

"Can you run?"

"I been hurt worse'n this playin' catch with my kids, course I kin run—it's jist a scratch, Brad." Ving gave him a wry look.

"What about you three?" Charlie and Pete nodded, but Jared was still holding his hands over his ears. Brad grabbed him by the shoulder and forced the man to look him in the eye. Brad pointed a forefinger at him and then made the symbol for "okay" with his thumb and forefinger. Jared nodded, albeit painfully, then made a circular motion with his own forefinger at his right ear.

"Go!" Brad made his fist-pumping motion again and pointed in the general direction of the aircraft. Jessica and Vicky, who had been looking back, turned and herded the hostages into a line. Jessica took the lead with Vicky taking up the trail position.

Shaken by the brutality and bloodshed he had just seen, Lamsam followed quickly behind Vicky. *If I manage to survive long enough to get back to that airplane, I have got Bykov! I am not sure how I'm going to account for the fact that I allowed the shooting to start, but I can honestly say that Bykov's troops initiated it—at least, that is the way I saw it. That is not precisely true, but who will dispute me? My report to the chief inspector will have to be ... abridged ... but it will not be the first time I have had to omit certain salient facts to lock up a case. I do believe my conscience will not trouble me.* He hurried after the hostages, his borrowed shotgun at the ready. For the first time since he had met Brad Jacobs, he had no doubt in his mind that he would use lethal force in the event it became necessary to defend a handful of foreign women who had recently transformed from hostages to witnesses. Bykov would be rotting in Bang Kwang Central Prison before the week was out.

"Move along as fast as you can, Jess. I have no doubt they'll be after us shortly." Brad tapped Ving on the chest and then tapped his own chest, meaning he wanted Ving to stay with him. Then he motioned for Charlie, Pete, and Jared to follow the women. It was an order they were reluctant to follow, but they grudgingly obeyed, although they moved at a slower pace than the women and they were continually looking back over their shoulders.

Brad ejected the magazine from his American 180 and inserted a fresh one. "How you fixed for ammo?"

Ving peered down into his chest pack and then looked back up at Brad, holding up his hand with four fingers extended. Brad checked his own chest pack, removed three drums, and shared them with

Ving. "We got to get moving, buddy, those bastards will be coming after us."

"Been a long time since I've seen anybody that crazy, Brad. Watchin' 'em come through that door that way an' walking over the bodies of their friends put me in mind a them freakin' jihadists." Ving was already backing in the direction the women had traveled, his eyes locked on the east wall of the monastery.

Brad followed suit, his own eyes sweeping from side to side. *We did not have enough intel for this mission. We've been damned lucky none of us was killed, and we're not out of the woods yet. For all I know, Bykov could have more of his security people stashed somewhere outside the monastery. Fly did not spot any, but all she had was the satellite photographs. That she did not pick up the heat signature is a plus, but it is no substitute for boots on the ground. We just didn't have time to do a proper recon dammit!*

He shook his head as if to clear it, expecting an onslaught from the direction of the monastery at any moment.

* * *

"Where are they now?" Bykov was livid, his voice thunderous as he slammed his fist onto his desk.

Red-faced, Mikhail threw up his hands in disgust and shame. "I've lost them. I don't know how I did it, but I've lost them."

"*Matyeryebyets!* What do you mean you've lost them? They were just in the supply corridor! There is only one way out of that corridor and it is double locked and guarded!" *They have taken the women...*

Mikhail had never seen the man so furious. He closed his eyes and forced himself to stop trembling. When Bykov was even mildly disturbed, underlings died, and Mikhail knew that was all he was to the Russian, an underling. His hands dropped to his keyboard. He punched a sequence of keys that brought up all the security camera feeds in the monastery on screen simultaneously. He used his mouse to move the cursor over the feed from the supply corridor and blanched. *Holy shit!*

Nausea threatened to overwhelm him. None of his classes at Northwestern had prepared him for this, and his subsequent service with Bykov in Eastern Europe and even here in Thailand had not prepared him for the carnage he was now witnessing. He had been fortunate to avoid getting a glimpse of the massacre of the monks who had occupied the monastery before. Bykov had left him at Pleasures until the renovations had been nearly completed. Mikhail Orel had not been called in until construction began on the communications center.

"Find them! Now!" *That's impossible! This monastery is impenetrable! It would have taken a large force to wreak that kind of havoc. Impossible!*

*Mikhail is more than competent, he is an expert with the electronics, and he is the most vigilant operator I have. How could a force with that kind of firepower simply materialize inside my fortress? Impossible!*

Bykov's iron will exerted itself, and he took a dozen deep breaths. *There is no such thing as magic. Losing my temper now will resolve nothing. More importantly, I need to keep Mikhail calm; I need his skills more than ever right now.*

"Mikhail, bring up all the outside cameras onscreen. Sooner or later they have to come out." *They did not come here to retake the monastery, this is a rescue attempt, nothing more ... but what kind of men are these? Who are they? My Zhonghu Rénmín Jiěfàngjūn tèzhǒng bùduì have been hand-picked from among some of the most elite fighters in the world, and these people have swept through them as easily as a knife cuts through butter!*

"Mikhail! How many of these men did you see? Were they wearing uniforms like professional soldiers?"

"No sir, they weren't wearing uniforms, and they were carrying weapons I'm not familiar with."

Bykov cocked his head to one side. "Oh?"

"They were carrying shotguns, sir, only they weren't like any shotguns I've ever seen. They had large magazines." Orel spread his hands apart to indicate the size. "And I would swear they were firing full automatic."

"Strange. I'm not familiar with a fully automatic shotgun. I've never heard of a military unit employing such a weapon."

Sensing the slightest softening of Bykov's rage, something he might be able to use to his advantage, Orel offered another little tidbit. "The shotguns were not the instruments that caused so much slaughter, sir. That was done by two men."

"This is not the time for hyperbole, Mikhail."

"It's not hyperbole, sir. There was a massive black man, sir, a man so dark that his skin looked blue in the lights of the corridor. He was firing a weapon that looked very much like a Tommy gun from World War II, only the barrel was very small, tiny in fact. The rest was done by one of the men carrying one of the automatic shotguns, but it was he who tossed two fragmentation grenades into the reinforcements."

"Two men?" Bykov shook his head in disbelief. "You're trying to tell me that *two men* killed thirty or so of the toughest fighting men on Earth?"

Orel shrugged then located the video and replayed it for Bykov.

"*Matyeryebyets!*" Bykov was astonished. After a moment, he spoke. "Locate Moroz. Have him round up as many of the reserve as he can and get them outside. Have someone assemble a platoon and get them into that supply corridor instantly!"

Orel spoke into his throat mic as his fingers flew across the keyboard. "Sir! Look at this!"

Irritated at the interruption, Bykov nevertheless stood up and walked over to look at Orel's main monitor. A man stood behind the redhead and the other hostages. He watched as the blonde girl, Jessica something, if he remembered correctly, and an Asian man bent over in the corridor and ran their fingers over something on the wall. A moment later a crack appeared in the seemingly solid wall, and, amazingly, a door slowly opened. "*Matyeryebyets!*"

\* \* \*

He knew that Jessica was an Olympic class distance runner. "Jess! Go on ahead, don't wait for us. Pete! Tell her how to get on board the aircraft and where you hid the magnetos." Jessica understood what her cousin was thinking instantly. She already had her private pilot's license, and she had watched Pete go through the startup procedure on the Martin PBM-5 in Jakarta. "Gotcha!" She stopped. "So where's the airplane?"

"Pete! Give her your monitor! Fly! Send her a map!" Brad barked his orders tersely.

Jessica turned and let Vicky take the head of the little column of hostages as she ran back to Pete.

The entire team was working in unison like the well-oiled machine that Team Dallas was known to be.

Having heard Brad, Pete quickly explained how to open the access door under the cockpit window and then told her the location of the secret compartment where he had hidden the magnetos. "You remember the startup procedure?"

"Pretty sure I do."

"Doesn't matter, Jess. The preflight checklist is in my Jepsen case. The startup procedure checklist is in there too." He gave her his pocket monitor.

"Got it!"

As she turned to begin her foot race to the lake, Pete had three words for her. "Good luck, kid!"

\* \* \*

It felt good to run again. Jessica quickly established a rhythm, arms, legs, lungs all working in perfect synchronicity. Fly had transmitted a topographical map to Pete's monitor, and the path down to the lake was clearly marked. The route was over rough terrain, but it was mostly downhill. The moment Jessica crested the peak she extended her stride and picked up speed. The sun was rising, and visibility was pretty good. The only thing that gave her any trouble was a slight tenderness in the ankle she had injured in Wyoming. *"Suck it up, girl!*

*You have run further than this with a hairline fracture; this is no time to wimp out!"*

\* \* \*

Sunan Lamsam stopped in his tracks and stared back at Brad. "What just happened?"

"Jess is going to start the aircraft."

"I don't—" He didn't get another word out of his mouth. At that exact moment a shot rang out. Professional instincts and years of experience sent Lamsam to the ground. He heard the massive burst of explosions from Pete's AA-12 and covered his head.

"Keep 'em moving, Vicky!" Brad stepped forward and offered Inspector Lamsam his hand. "Patrol," he said by way of explanation. "I forgot about those."

Lamsam suppressed a retort. *I cannot fault the man. I knew about the patrols as well. This has not turned out quite the way I expected. I am afraid I have not contributed as much to this operation as I could have. I shall have to find some way to repay these men. From this day forward I will have a higher opinion of American Marines. I have never met men quite like these.*

Brad turned his head suddenly, facing the rear. "Did you hear that?" He could hear shouts and the steady drumbeat of boots on the ground in the distance. "They heard the shots and they've found our back trail! Vicky, faster!" Without another word, he began to run again, increasing his pace, though not as much as he wanted to. The hostages weren't moving fast enough.

\* \* \*

As soon as Jessica climbed in through the access door beneath the cockpit window, she raced to the secret compartment and removed the magnetos. Still dripping wet from her swim, she opened the double cargo doors, locking them in the open position.

Engine number one sputtered to life reassuringly. The characteristic rough startup idle smoothed out, and Jessica initiated the startup procedure for engine number two. The big 2100 horsepower Pratt & Whitney engine coughed twice and the propeller came to a standstill. Jessica felt the panic rise in her gut. She could hear Brad and the others screaming into their earwigs. Bykov's security personnel had apparently heard one of the AA-12s go off and had immediately uncovered the team's back trail. From what she could hear, she assumed that the hostiles were catching up to them quickly.

Her first instinct was to cry out to Pete, but she fought back the urge. As Brad had taught her years before, she centered herself by taking ten deep breaths. Then she wracked her brain, searching her memory for causes and remedies for an engine misfire. After a moment, she grabbed the throttle handles for engine number two and backed them off just a tad. The starter seemed to drag just a little, and the propeller turned very slowly. Just as she was about to disengage the starter, the engine coughed and sputtered into life. It took a minute or so for the idle to smooth out, but soon both engines were roaring smoothly. The fuselage of the huge aircraft was vibrating encouragingly, and Jessica backed off the throttles on both engines.

"We're getting close, Jess!" Vicky sounded a little winded. Jessica heard the familiar bark of AK-47s in her earwig, followed by the distinctive buzz of the two American 180s and the thunder of the AA-12s.

"They backin' up, Brad!" She heard Ving's deep southern drawl in her ear.

"They're just regrouping."

"This may be the last chance we get," she heard Jared shout.

"Go for it!" That was Vicky shouting at the hostages.

Jessica could sense the urgency in the voices of her team members and she knew she had to take a chance on taxiing the big Martin in closer to shore. She'd not been strong enough to offload the RB-15 by herself.

"Pile up all the explosive ordnance across the path—leave it in the rucksacks, no time to try to conceal it!" The last hundred yards or so to the lake had been a broad dirt path leading to a short but rickety pier, so she knew Brad and the others were extremely close. She aimed the nose of the Martin at the end of the pier. Everyone would get soaked, but that was better than being shot at. Just as the nose of the Martin bumped against the ramshackle pier, Jess heard an enormous blast, followed by the terrified screaming of the hostages. Bits of debris from the explosion rained down on the fuselage, causing Jessica to wince.

She could no longer hear voices in her earwig, no one was talking. There was a lot of rapid breathing and the sounds of splashing.

* * *

Vicky was by far the fastest swimmer on the team, and she reached the Martin well ahead of the others. Despite her superb physical condition, lifting herself through the open cargo door and up onto the deck of the aircraft proved extremely difficult. Her wet clothing—the terrycloth robe bearing Pleasures' monogrammed logo that she had thrown on when Brad and the team had arrived to rescue her—seemed to weigh a ton. She lay down on the deck, her arms and shoulders hanging over the edge so that she could reach down and help the hostages aboard the aircraft. Jared swam around the spluttering and gasping women and lifted himself aboard so that he could help Vicky pull them out of the water.

*Track Down Thailand*

Pete had swum around to the access door beneath the cockpit window and, despite his injuries, had clambered up and into the cockpit. He didn't acknowledge Jessica, sitting in the copilot's seat, until he had buckled himself into his own seat.

"Are they aboard yet?" He was reaching for the throttles even as he asked the question.

Jessica twisted around and looked through the cockpit door to see Brad lifting Inspector Lamsam up into the aircraft. Kneeling on one knee, Jared lifted his right hand, thumb up, to signal that all were aboard. "Go!" Jessica all but screamed. She swiveled around and looked past Pete's dripping bulk and out the cockpit window. Several of the black-clad Chinese were approaching the shore of the lake, but most were limping or injured in some way. There was a large pile of bodies back near a blackened spot at the start of the dirt path.

Pete shoved the throttle on the starboard engine forward to full military power and the Martin heeled over to starboard as it spun like a child's top. The instant the nose of the craft pointed out into open water, Pete shoved the throttle for the port side engine all the way forward and the nose of the aircraft lifted with the thrust. For what seemed like an eternity, the forward motion was sluggish, hellishly slow. A hail of bullets peppered the aluminum skin of the fuselage, leaving holes that Jessica could actually see through. She said a fervent prayer that none of them would do any real damage.

\* \* \*

Sunan Lamsam was struggling to keep his voice steady as he spoke into the cell phone Brad had returned to him once the aircraft was moving. A newer model, the cell phone was working even though the plastic bag Brad had sealed it in had been compromised at some point and water had leaked in.

Brad listened as Lamsam related, in Thai, an abbreviated report to his chief inspector, giving details, including coordinates for the monastery and the fact that he had access to video corroborating most of the salient facts of his report. When he finished, there had been a pause, and Brad had watched as Lamsam's face reflected a gamut of emotions. Then he heard Lamsam in English.

"Yes sir! They are sitting right here beside me." Lamsam activated the video camera in his cell phone and directed it at the bedraggled former hostages, who were still sobbing from relief and shock. In moments Lamsam shut down the video and spoke into the cell phone again. "Yes sir! I will check with the pilot and get an estimated time of arrival. Yes sir, right away, sir!"

He turned to Brad. "I have been given an order, but I feel compelled to put it to you as a request from the chief inspector. I respectfully request that you direct Pete to fly to Bangkok as quickly as possible, and I also request that you give me an estimated time of arrival. The chief inspector has given me his word that if I can establish the facts of my report to his satisfaction he will grant you immunity from prosecution." He paused for a moment, looking Brad directly in the eyes. "There will be a short delay in your departure from Bangkok, but you will be honored guests of the Royal Thai government while we secure the monastery—and Bykov—and the witnesses are interviewed by our prosecutors."

"I appreciate you framing that as a request, but I take it that is more in the nature of an order, is it not?"

Lamsam lowered his eyelids and spoke with what seemed to be the utmost sincerity. "From one Marine to another, I give you my word. I have known the chief inspector all of my life. He is an honorable man, and I have never known him to lie.

If he says he will grant you immunity from prosecution, he will do so."

"I'm going to have to take you at your word, inspector—I have a hunch that jets from the Royal Thai Air Force have already been scrambled and are on their way to intercept us."

Lamsam sighed and nodded his head in the affirmative.

# Epilogue

## Don Muang Royal Thai Air Force Base

Team Dallas stood on the tarmac outside the Base Operations Building at Don Muang Royal Thai Air Force Base, 40 kilometers north of Central Bangkok, watching as the ungainly C-130 Hercules touched down on the main runway. A battalion of Royal Thai Marines had been deployed to the monastery, expecting to lay siege to the ancient stone building. Instead, they had found a vastly understrength security force, one that had been decimated by forces unknown. Only a few members of the Royal Thai Police Special Branch forensics team sent to the monastery with the Marines had any idea of who had so effectively dismantled Bykov's elite security force, and they had been ordered to keep their mouths shut.

The Marine battalion commander was baffled by the statements collected by his S–2 (Intelligence)

Section to the effect that the carnage inflicted on the security force had been accomplished by a team of no more than six men. The Marines had rounded up the remnants of the security force with little or no opposition, but Bykov had not been found. Several other Russian nationals had put up some resistance in the communications center deep within the bowels of the monastery. When they had compromised the heavy steel door to the communications center, there had been a brief firefight, and they had stopped one Mikhail Orel in the act of destroying a very sophisticated and expensive computer system.

The Russians and the remnants of the security force had been disarmed and locked away in the former monks' cells in the corridor that had only recently been their barracks, pending their handover to the judicial system of the Royal Thai government. A radar scan located a rather large commercial helicopter making a beeline for the Laotian border at high speed. Fighter jets had been dispatched immediately to force it down. Bykov had been taken into custody and loaded onto a C-130, the one Team Dallas was waiting for.

* * *

"I don't think I've ever seen an investigation, trial, and conviction accomplished in the space of three days before." Brad and Inspector Lamsam were sitting at a table poolside at the Mandarin Oriental Hotel in Bangkok, where the Royal Thai government had so graciously lodged Team Dallas for the duration of the trial. Vicky and Jessica were sunning themselves a few feet away, and Ving, Jared, and Pete were leaning up against the poolside bar sipping ice-cold Singha beers and ogling the scantily clad waitresses. Charlie had gone to meet Kiet Benjawan at the rented warehouse in Pattaya City to thank him for the logistical support and to return the vehicles.

"Justice in this country is meted out rather swiftly, my friend. I know it is far different in your country, but our system meets our needs rather handsomely."

"You have no appeals process?"

Lamsam shrugged. "There is no need for an appeal. Bykov clearly violated some of our most sacred laws. The evidence you and your team gathered is incontrovertible, and the hostages you rescued were highly credible. What is there to appeal?"

* * *

The sleek, two-engine Airbus A350 touched down at Dallas-Fort Worth International Airport so gently that Vicky's head never stirred from its resting place on Brad's shoulder.

*I should never have let her or Jess talk me into this mission. I know better than to take on a mission without adequate intelligence. Money be damned, it's not worth the risk. If I thought it would do any good, I might try to talk them out of their involvement in Team Dallas altogether ... but that would be a complete waste of time. I can't change either of them, they're born warriors.*

He sighed and reached over to shake Vicky's shoulder. "We're home, babe."

## THE END.

*Thank you for taking the time to read TRACK DOWN THAILAND. If you enjoyed it, please consider telling your friends or posting a [short review](). Word of mouth is an author's best friend and much appreciated. Thank you, Scott Conrad.*

A BRAD JACOBS THRILLER SERIES

**TRACK DOWN AFRICA – BOOK 1**
**TRACK DOWN ALASKA – BOOK 2**
**TRACK DOWN AMAZON – BOOK 3**
**TRACK DOWN IRAQ – BOOK 4**
**TRACK DOWN BORNEO – BOOK 5**
**TRACK DOWN EL SALVADOR – BOOK 6**
**TRACK DOWN WYOMING – BOOK 7**
**TRACK DOWN THAILAND – BOOK 8**

ScottConradBooks.com

Printed in Great Britain
by Amazon